CONTENTS

Intro.	3
Day 1	5
Day 2	14
Day 3	22
Day 4	29
Day 5	35
Day 6	42
Day 7	55
Day 8	75
Day 9	88
Day 10	95
Day 11	105
Day 12	113
Day 13	119
Day 14	132
Day 15	138
Day 16	152

Day 17	171
Postscript	178
Acknowledgement	181

17 Days
By
Michael J May

INTRO.

Meet Jack; 41 years young, has 2 wonderful kids, a lovely wife, and basically a great life. But it wasn't always this way. This book basically is a day-by-day account of the 17 days leading up to the finalisation of his divorce. Why just those 17 days? Well, they contained the lowest & highest points of the whole period; life was complicated. And Shit. But, mostly complicated. And Shit. I could have written about any time during that period to be honest, because it was all shite. But these 17 will do.

It may come across as chaotic at times, but that's exactly how it was in those days. Written to be both realistic and a bit funny, it shows the state of mind he was in. It goes from Story to Tangents quite a bit. The Tangents go a bit more into the details/emotional shiteness of the whole process.

And, let's face it, nobody ever cares about how divorce affects men. It's always all about the woman, naturally assumed to be the victim. We all know that's not always true, so I wanted to get the male perspective across. Which is the important message here; men don't always have it easy during divorces.

There are exceptions to the rule, but a lot of us suffer in silence; too proud or scared to get help. And, although this book is a work of fiction, it is based on some true-life experiences.

Don't suffer in silence, there are people out there to talk to.

Guys, this book is for you.

DAY 1

Saturday, 1st of March.

How did I end up in this situation? The question went through my mind like a hurricane. Unable to stop the whirlwind of madness, I changed into my running kit and went out into the cold. Running always seemed to make me feel better and cleared my mind of all the badness in my life. And there was plenty of that at the moment; a divorce imminent. Today was March 1st, and the decree absolute was due on the 17th. 17 days until I could put this nightmare behind me or try to do so at least. It had been a nightmare; solicitor's letters, heated phone calls, financial back and forth. How did I end up in this situation? Ugh, the question came back. Time to get outside and clear my head. I closed the front door behind me, after checking for the fifth time that I had my key. "Alright Jack" My neighbour, just about to go inside after getting home from work. "Alright mate" I responded. Thankfully, he unlocked his door and went inside. No prolonged awkward conversation, thanks mate. A divorcee himself, he likely understood that I didn't really want to talk about it. He knew what was going on of course, most of the road did. Gossip spreads like wildfire in a village like this. Katie and he had split up the year before after she left him. Took his kids, and most of his money. Something I was dreading, but we hadn't worked out the details just yet.

A creature of habit, my run would be along the canal tow path, which was close to my house. It was ideal for running; flat enough for my old man fitness, and the scenery always took my mind of whatever was going on in my head. I pressed the buttons on my Fenix watch and did a bit of stretching whilst it located satellites. Weird how it always managed that within seconds when I first got it, but now seems to take longer and longer. See? Already working as my mind is on something else! Brilliant. My watch finally beeped to let me know it was ready, so I pressed the start button and set off down the tow path. Felt good; the weather was cold, but pleasant. The path was dry, and there weren't a lot of people out at the moment. After about 10 minutes, I started to falter a little, but knew I just had to plod on. Most people get into their stride after a mile or so; with me it takes about 5k. Which was unfortunate as I only do 5k runs. I could easily carry on, but I have this thing in my head that if I stick to

5k's, my knees won't get damaged. True or not, it was hard-set in my mind, so I stick to it. Haven run the same route for a few years now, I knew exactly when I had to turn back so my route was as close to 5k as possible. There was a fine mist on the canal, no boat movements, and only a handful of fishermen on the opposite bank. The sounds of nature around me, helping to clear my head. No headphones for me. Can't do it. Tried it a few times, but the differing beats in songs made me run faster/slower, messing up my routine. And Lord knows, I do love a good routine.

Made it home in nearly the same time as yesterday. Did my usual; got a bottle of drink, sat on the doorstep, uploaded my running stats, and just chilled. The old lady from 4 doors up was walking off in the opposite direction, with her yappy little dog. I'm not a dog person, just to make that clear from the outset. I prefer cats; easier to look after. They don't need walking, can use a toilet, and are generally low maintenance. Weird how dog owners can't understand that there are people out there that don't actually like dogs. It's like you're some sort of freak. I'm not a freak, just don't like dogs. No apologies offered. (Or needed!). Finished my drink and had a shower. Nice long, hot shower. My mind was still in a good place. Let's try and keep it there! Dressed, and went down to get myself a coffee. Whilst I was making my coffee, my day collapsed; the postman put something through the letterbox. Shit. My heart sank, I knew there would be something to drag me back down into deep despair. I took a deep breath and went to see what was delivered. A single letter lay on the doormat, not official looking; a personal letter. Who sends letters these days I thought as I picked it up. Ah, recognition. My wife's handwriting. She has to communicate via letters now?? What the?? I sat at the kitchen table, sipped my coffee, staring at the letter in front of me. Here are the thoughts going through my mind (in no particular order, envisage a hurricane of questions):

1. What does she want?

2. Bitch

3. Is there something wrong?

4. Bitch

5. Is she trying to make up?

6. Bitch

7. Does she have unrelated bad news?

8. Bitch

9. Is it related to the kids?

10. Bitch

11. What does she want? No, wait, I did that one already.

12. Bitch

Going around my mind like a confusing

whirlwind, scary, anxious, annoying.

I finished my coffee and took a deep breath. *Just do it. Go. Now. Do it. Get on with it. What are you afraid of?* (Well, see above obviously dumbass) I picked it up, and checked the back; no return address. I knew she was shacked up with that arsehole but I had no idea where exactly. She obviously didn't want me to know. And, to be honest, I didn't really want to know. What difference would it make? She had my kids, shacked up with some loser, being all happy somewhere. Knowing where they were would make no difference. I berated myself for drifting off course and opened the envelope.

Single sheet, not even half full, just a few lines. "Jack," Wait, not even "Dear Jack", or "Hi Jack", just "Jack". Fuck. Very aggressive start. I scanned the 5 lines of text, no asking how I was etc. She basically wanted me out of the house for an afternoon so she could come and choose what she wanted to take from the house. If there was anything specific I didn't want her to take, could I please let her know. She wouldn't take anything that was mine, just stuff like furniture, crockery etc.

Anyways, read for yourself, and make your own mind up.

Jack,

I would like to collect my belongings, and

possibly some furniture. If there are specific bit and pieces you don't want me to take, please let me know. I was hoping to do this one afternoon next week. Could you please let me know when is best? I think it's probably a good idea if there was nobody home, as I don't want to get into any arguments.

Helen.

Angry thoughts raced around immediately; who the hell did she think she was? Looking around MY house without me there?? I paced around the kitchen, full of anger. Grrrrrr! My day ruined already, and it was only 07.40. Ffs. But then, suddenly, I stopped. I looked at the letter and envelope again. What an idiot. How am I supposed to respond? No return address, and she had blocked me on her mobile, so I couldn't text or WhatsApp her.

Genius, that made me feel better! And worried at the same time. And, to make it even better, I had changed the locks, so she couldn't get in without me letting her in. I changed the locks front and back a few weeks ago, as she sent me a message one day saying she'd been in to get some more clothes. Well, I wasn't having that, was I? How dare she just come into my house! MY FUCKING HOUSE! She had already made it clear that she wanted half the equity in the house. Half! For what? She wasn't on the mortgage, so couldn't force me to sell up thankfully. But, even then, she'd never contributed towards the mortgage, and I did all the DIY. How could she possibly be entitled to half the equity in the house??

My solicitor friend had advised me that it was legitimately legal (yeah legitimately legal, it's a thing), and my choice was to either sell up, or re-mortgage. *Hang on, knob.* Here I was telling you about the letter, and I've gone off on a tangent about the house! Though, I feel like I need to finish talking about the house now, instead of leaving it hanging. So, anyways, I took his advice, and looked at a re-mortgage. I had 10 years left on my mortgage, and that would go back up to 25 years in order to afford to give her half of the equity (which would be £35k). 35K, as it happened, would in reality cost me £47k. I hate her. I really do.

Anyhoo, the letter. Yeah, so in order to cover myself, I picked up my phone, rang her number (blocked, so didn't connect), send a text (failed), sent WhatsApp message (not received). Done. If it ever came up, I could just show them my phone to prove I had tried to get in touch with her, but she'd blocked me, and I had no comms avenue open to me. Not sure what else I was supposed to do. Checked the clock, 08.09! Time to go. I had arranged to meet my mate Steve to help him move house. Small village, so he wasn't going far, so would be pretty easy. And a welcome distraction. In a better mood, I got my stuff, put my coat on, and left the house.

I spent most of the day helping Steve out, which was great! Hard work, and quality time spent with an old friend. He didn't ask about the divorce, thankfully. We had a bit of fun, and I left to go home in a great mood! Drove to Sainsbury's (local, not huge) in Ramsey on the way home and picked up a pizza and a couple bottles of Porter. Not a great diet, but I had worked hard today. Got home, it was starting to get cold, so I put the heating on. Chucked pizza in the oven, and beer in the freezer.

When it was done, I parked myself, then caught up on some YouTube videos, then a couple of episodes of 24. I had watched all series of 24 years before but found that I needed something to keep me occupied since this whole shit business had started. I'd forgotten how good 24 was. Though we shared a first name, Bauer was nothing like me. Or, I was nothing like him to be more precise and fairer. Bauer was confident, strong, and could fight just about anybody. Me? Negative confidence and strength. And sub-zero on the fight front; had never had a fight in my life.

I picked up a guitar and played random stuff whilst watching. Poured my Porter, which was nice. (Yeah, Fast Show reference!) Not had this one before, oooh, how exciting my life was!!! Watched a couple of episodes, then my eyes started to fail me. Bedtime.

Couldn't be bothered to do the dishes (unusual for me), too tired. Put the cat out (much to her dismay!), fed her, made sure she had water, and went to bed. None of the usual demons came to keep me awake that night, and I fell into a deep sleep. A welcome change from the sleepless nights I had been having the last few weeks.

DAY 2

Sunday, 2nd of March.

I opened my eyes slowly, expecting to see an obscene time on the alarm clock. To my surprise, however, I focussed in and saw it was 07.43. Eh? A record surely! This day was starting off great! Yeah! I stretched, got out of bed, and went to the loo. Ran my head under a cold tap, then changed into my running gear, and opened the curtains; I wasn't to be disappointed by the weather either! Sun was just coming up, and it was dry. Legendary. Happy, I trotted downstairs, has a quick drink of pineapple juice, and set off to repeat my daily routine. No neighbour this time, no fishermen either; it was too early for most thankfully. I ran along the tow path, quite happy, lost in my awesomeness, when……
A dog ran out of the trees, straight at me! "Fuck! Shit! Bollocks!" I shouted instinctively. Dog jumping up at me, barking. Bloody dogs. I looked

around to see if I could find and berate the owner, when a very charming lady emerged from the trees. She was out of breath, running towards the dog.

"Oh my God, I'm so sorry! Chico! Down!" She took the dog by the collar and pulled it away from me. "Are you ok? I'm so sorry. The lead snapped, and he ran off into the woods." I took a moment, thinking to myself how fit she was, then responded.

"Uhm, yeah, I'm ok. No harm done." There was no harm done, I just shit myself (not literally), and just didn't like dogs. I think the latter may have come across as obvious, because she started explaining that the dog wasn't hers, and that she was just visiting her aunt and took her dog for a walk, and, and … I waved my hands and told her it was really ok. She apologised again, and I told her it was ok. Again. She started dragging the dog back towards the village, and I set off in the opposite direction.

I ran along, thinking I had not seen her anywhere before. I lived in a small village, and thought I knew ("knew" by sight, not personally) almost everyone around here. *Wait, are you kidding Jack? You know hardly anyone in the village!* Yeah, true, I don't. I didn't know many people really. Damn you inner voice!! It was winter, and fairly quiet in the village. Not that we got particularly busy in the warmer months, but still got our fair share of tourists. The village was very pretty with its thatched roofs, charming old pub, and small quay side. This made it an ideal stop off for the various canal boat tourists. I don't mind it, as it kept the local businesses alive. Local trade was ok, but the tourists just gave the boost that made them a little extra money.

Anyways, where was I? Drifting again. Ah yeah. So, I carried on with my usual run, then sat on the front step with my drink, uploading my run.

"Oh, hi again!" What? I looked up, and there she was again. With dog but tied to the lead with a rather crude looking knot.

"Oh hi" I said. The dog jumped up, and sniffed at the air, like it could smell something that piqued its interest. I heard the cat running away down the hall behind me. I petted the dog on the head (out of politeness more than anything) and kind of pointed over my shoulder

"Cat" I said.

"Ah, that's what he's so interested in" she replied with a laugh. My god, I thought, she's beautiful. Not in a supermodel way, but in more of a classic beauty kind of way. The smile really lit up her face and filled me with a strange sort of feeling of calm. Chico, disappointed at the cat's disappearance, started pulling her away up the road. "Wow! Sorry, looks like he wants to get home! Bye again!" she said as she was being dragged up the road.

"Bye" I said with a wave, not sure if she heard me. Don't think she did, she turned her head and stumbled off around the corner, after the dog. I sat for a while, partially to cool down, partially in the hope that she would come back. She didn't, obviously. I went back in, showered, and changed.

I'm not going to lie; I hadn't even thought about another woman for years. Even after the hell of Helen leaving me, I hadn't given it a thought. I was almost resigned to spending the rest of my life alone, which would probably work well for me to be honest. I was quite happy with my own company. Oh, and here I am, thinking ahead of myself; I had only just met this woman, and didn't even know her. Why was I already thinking about a new relationship? An odd feeling, considering I wasn't ready to let go of Helen. *Yes, I was*. No, I wasn't. *Yes, I was*. Wasn't I? Wasn't I?? Grrrr! WTF? *Yes, you are! She's a bitch remember?*

Nothing else planned for the day, I decided to clean the house, top to bottom. Yeah, that would be good. Oh, wait, I did that last Sunday. But I did it anyway. The house was immaculate, literally just a coffee cup by the sink. Nobody here to make a mess. This sent me off on a downward spiral. My kids. Oh my God, how I missed them. I hadn't seen them for 4 days now, and it was killing me. I spent the last few weeks crying myself to sleep. Not having my kids around made me profoundly sad. I'd never known anything like it. "Stop it!" I shouted out loud at myself, cursing my weakness. Stay positive. Ffs, man up. Right, fuck it, I'm off out.

Closing the door behind me, I looked at my watch. I had just walked out of the house, no idea where I was going. It was 15.07 on a Sunday. Where was I going?? Shit. Erm. Ah! Pub. Yeah, pub. Not to get pissed, but to get a Sunday roast. And beer. Obviously. Wait! Patting my pockets desperately, I thankfully found my door key. Relax man! I gathered myself, looked around (nobody saw), and walked off in the direction of the pub. Damned anxiety.

The George Inn is a traditional pub, with a few (mostly local) real ales on tap, and a fantastic menu. Jason, who ran the pub, had struck gold when he took on a chef that worked absolute magic in the kitchen. All traditional fayre mid, but soooooo good. I walked in and ordered a pint at the bar. It had been a few weeks since I had been here, and Jason commented as such.

"Yeah, having a bit of a rough time" I explained. He nodded knowingly (did fucking EVERYONE know what was going on in my life??) I took my pint and looked around for a table. Spotted one in the corner and made my way towards it. I had just sat down and was about to take a sip of my pint, when I saw someone sat over by the window. It was her. Shit. She was talking to an older lady, her aunt presumably. Just as I was looking, she turned her head and saw me. She waved over enthusiastically "Hi again!" I felt like a teenager that got caught

staring, and I'm sure I was blushing. Shit, shit, shit! I just waved back. She turned back to the old lady, and they started talking, with the occasional point/nod in my direction. Feeling a bit self-conscious, I got up to order my food at the bar. Jason smiled and asked if I knew her.
"No" I said, "Do you?"
"She's Mary's niece"
"Who?" I asked.
"Mary, lives opposite the post office" I still didn't know who she was, but just said "Ah" and ordered my food. I mentally prepared myself, then turned and walked back to my table. Sadly, I looked over, and saw that they had left. Disappointed. *Disappointed? Why? You don't know her. Why would you be disappointed?* But I was. Dejected, I ate my roast beef (which was superb by the way) and walked home.

After I left the pub, I found myself unintentionally walking home via the post office. *What are you doing?? That's just super obvious!* But, regardless, I carried on, and as I walked by the post office, I looked across to see if I could work out where Mary lived. I saw nothing obvious and managed to walk by unnoticed. Slightly dejected, I walked the rest of the way lost in thoughts of the divorce. Shit. Need to do something to get my mind off it. Got home, filled up my water bottle, and turned on the pc & lost myself in a game. My head was already starting to ache, so I drank more water.

For some reason, over the last few years, I got a headache after just one pint. It was weird, but probably caused by not drinking water throughout the day I thought. Hence, I have to make sure I drink water before bed, or I'll be awake with a sore head all night. Naturally, I had to get up a couple of times in the night for a pee, but rather that than pain. Anyway, erm, ah yeah. Gaming. So, got to the point where I was just losing all the time, so I shut down the pc.

Checked my watch; 23.46, time for bed. Had a pee, did my teeth, and got into bed. Sigh. Because of the shit I was in, I had issues switching off & falling asleep. Every time I closed my eyes, thoughts came thick & fast.

Bad thoughts, Sad thoughts.

Thoughts of my kids. I miss them so much.

Thoughts of self-loathing. Never good.....

I'd spoken about the sleeplessness with Steve, and he'd recommended I try audiobooks the app he'd mentioned came with a free download, so I downloaded it. Wow. So much choice! I browsed for a bit and eventually chose a Sherlock Holmes title that was 17hrs long. Genius. I would probably miss most of the stories, but if it helped, I didn't mind.

I set my alarm for the morning, and think I lasted

12 mins or so in Victorian London before I was out. And the world was a good place.

DAY 3

Monday, 3rd of March.

Tranquil music roused me from my sleep at 7, I had a stretch, and got up. Peeking through the curtains, I saw that the weather was still holding, but it looked cold. Genius, means I can go for a run before getting to work. Work, yeah, so what do I do for a living? Well, after years of working in Engineering, I decided it was time for a change of direction. I could see the growing trend in online content (think YouTube etc) and thought this would be just the thing for me. I started doing some night classes & got a few qualifications in digital content editing. Started off helping out some mates, and a few local businesses for free. Then out of the blue, I got an email from a musician I had never heard of. I checked him out and discovered he had quite a following on YouTube. He wanted to know if I would be willing to help enhance his videos. Apparently, one of his subscribers had recommended me to him. Not sure how that worked or happened, but I didn't care. He was willing to pay, so I agreed. I will say that his music isn't really to my liking, but that doesn't really matter when you're editing/creating content. This was 2 years ago now, and I've gained 4 more clients via this guy since then; life is good.

Was good.

Divorce. Ffs.

Anyways, that's what I do for a living. I have a home office setup in the loft and spend most of my day up there. It's my happy place, a place where the outside world doesn't exist. I love my job, so tend to get totally lost in it, losing track of time completely. Which, let's face it, really helps these days. Today was no exception. I went for a run, showered, changed, and got to work. I stopped occasionally, just to make myself a coffee. Some of the videos this week cover gear reviews, which are the more interesting ones to be honest. As a "guitarist" myself (loose term….), they pique my interest. Also, they require careful editing & review to ensure we don't insult/alienate perspective endorsements/sponsors. I had 4 of these to get through, to be released on Saturday morning, so I had to finish them Thursday for client review Friday. I know what you're thinking; surely there isn't that much to be made in editing videos. Well, you'd be surprised.

Fortunately for me, one of my clients (the one with 4 gear reviews this week) is an online musical instrument retailer. Nothing major league, but big enough to be able to afford to pay me. So, yeah, I make enough. On a par with my earnings as an Engineer? Getting there. A ways to go yet, but I was sure it would eventually... I have another big client in the pipeline, but I haven't mentioned that to anyone, as I want to leave anything like that until after the divorce is final.

So, finances. Yeah, a lot of people go through the courts to sort the financial side of a divorce out. But much to my surprise, she didn't want to do that. We came up with a fair monthly amount for me to pay her to cover the kids support etc. It was a lot, but not un-manageable. Basically, this new client would cover all that every month, so I was sort of ok with it. She doesn't know about that, but that's not a "me problem". There had been no mention of annual increases in the amount I paid monthly, so I was happy. I later found out that she also left me with a £1500 overdraft I was unaware of, and almost £3000 in credit card debt. This had made me very angry. Seriously angry. None of it was mine, it was all her, and she refused to pay anything towards it. She didn't work, so I was supporting her, and this is how she repaid me. Did I mention that she's a bitch? Yeah, I think I have. I should state that this was all BEFORE solicitor involvement, but I'll go into that later. Don't want to talk about that just yet, as it still makes me angry now.

Erm, anyways, my day, so, yeah, I worked till 5, and called it a day. I'd finished 6 videos and had about 12 left to do this week. All shortish ones. Comfortable. I felt good. Not a negative thought in sight. Nothing bad in the post, just random stuff. I went through the fridge and made myself some dinner. Nothing flashy, egg frittata with some broccoli. Simple, tasty. Checked my phone; messages from my mum, and from Steve. Nothing bad. Breathe. Mum, obviously worried, even though I was a grown man. "Mums don't stop worrying, no matter how old you are" she'd once said to me. I can believe it. Looking out of the window, I could see it was getting dark, but I wanted to get out for air. Cleaned up (house is at show home standard!) and headed out for a walk.

Jesus, it was getting colder. No particular route in mind, I wandered around the village. As I walked past the little supermarket, I was so lost in my own mind that I almost bumped into a lady coming out of the shop.
"Oh, I'm really sorry" I said genuinely.
"Not a problem" she responded. I apologised again and walked on.
"Excuse me, young man" *Eh? Me?* I turned and saw that yes; she did indeed mean me.
"Yes?" I said, slightly confused.

She walked over and said "You're the young man my Chrissy was talking about. We saw you in the George yesterday?" Instant recognition. And instant registration; Chrissy, that was her name.
"Ah yes, the girl from the tow path"
She smiled "Yes, I'm sorry if my dog bothered you. The lead broke, and he just ran off. He's normally no trouble at all".
"Don't worry, it was ok. Just startled me a bit was all" I chuckled.
"Sorry. It won't happen again though. Last thing we did before she went back home was to order a new lead online" *Wait, what? She's gone?? Shit.* Don't know why I was so upset over it; I barely knew her (if at all).
"Oh, she's gone home?" I asked, my disappointment thinly veiled.
"Yes, but she comes to see me regularly. She lives in the city but enjoys coming out here to escape the noise. And to see her favourite Aunt of course".
I smiled, not only because the old lady did, but also because I was secretly happy about the "regularly" part. *Lives in the city, eh?* The "city" was a local thing, referring to the town of Peterborough.

To put your wondering/questioning mind at ease, I should probably tell you that I live in a small village called Ramsey Forty Foot, so called as it lies on the Forty Foot Drain. Don't ask, just accept it as a quiet little village. To add further context: my soon to be ex-wife lives somewhere in the main village of Ramsey, about a mile and a half away. Doesn't have an impact on this story, but just "fyi" I suppose.

"Well, I won't take up any more of your time young man, I just wanted to say hello" she said.
"Please, it's Jack" I replied, "Young man sounds so formal".
She chuckled "Mary, pleased to meet you".
"Mary, very nice to meet you" I said, with a slight bow of the head.
"Have a pleasant evening, Jack" She smiled, turned, and started walked away
"Oh, Jack" she said, turning back. "She'll be back this weekend. In case you were wondering" She smiled, and walked off.

Well, I thought, there's a great end to my day. She's coming back; I felt like a teenager inside, all giddy & happy. I continued my walk in a daze, and eventually ended up back home. I'd lost all track of time; it was 1900 and dark. And cold. I went in, grabbed a beer, lit the fire, and watched a few episodes of 24.

I replayed the encounter with Mary a few times in my head, trying to see if there were any further details I could extract. There weren't. But, I had a name. Chrissy. That would do for now.

I tidied, and went to bed. Put headphones in, Holmes was just advising Watson to bring his

service revolver. Things may get nasty old chum.
No idea if the needed the revolver though, because:
Sleep came easy that night.
Tidy.

DAY 4

Tuesday, 4th of March.

The following morning found me in a great mood. The alarm went off, I got up, went for a quick run, showered, and got ready for another busy day of editing. I sat eating breakfast, my second cup of coffee in hand, checking my phone. Another day without bad emails; mostly from clients about the edits I sent out yesterday. A couple of tweaks were requested, which wouldn't take me long. I don't take offence when clients respond with comments on the edits. I expect them. Let's face it, I can't always give them exactly what they want, so I'm more than open to suggestions. Mostly there were minor things, and I was more than happy with that. Conversely, if I thought that the video would benefit from additions/re-shoots, I was more than comfortable making my thoughts known. Fortunately, my relationship with clients was excellent, and they trusted my input. Honesty is the best policy, as they say.

Or is it? Well, standby for another tangent.... Honesty. Hmmm. So, when Helen and I first discussed divorce. No wait, there was no discussion; she just told me quite plainly and matter-of-factly that she wanted to split up. Anyway, we discussed it loosely afterwards, in between me breaking down, and her getting very angry. Here's the long & short of it: she needed a reason for the divorce to put on the application. There was some back & forth regarding drifting apart, irreconcilable differences, etc. It was all getting VERY complicated and dragging on. She said they would recommend counselling and stuff before the application was approved. (Is that even true??????) In the end, I just blurted out "Just blame it on me, say I cheated on you". I hadn't, but just wanted to get it all over with. THAT was a decision I was to regret later on. Big time. NEVER do that. NEVER. I was an idiot, and still berate myself now. So, she agreed to that, and the papers were submitted & approved. Shit. Not so much that it was over, but that I had agreed to take the blame. Idiot. There was no Honesty involved here eh. It is the best policy, but it would have dragged this nightmare out longer than I could have taken mentally. So, I lied. And live to regret it every day.

Positives: it sped up the process. It was all approved & processed fairly rapidly. (Rapid = 8 months)

Negatives: Many. Personal loathing, and many other things. Plus, alienation by her family. I had a great relationship with my in-laws, and her two brothers. That all went away immediately. No contact from them whatsoever.

Over the years, that has thawed somewhat. I see her brothers around occasionally. At first, they totally ignored me, and her parents. Eventually, there was hello's etc. All very polite. Then perhaps a bit of chit chat. Never anything meaningful or anything though. Last year, after bumping into her parents occasionally, I decided I needed to set the record straight; I text her mother and told her that the reason for our divorce was because she had drifted away from me. Not because I had cheated on her, I had not done so. I have no idea how she reacted to the message, because she didn't respond, and sadly passed away a few months after. But I take some comfort in the fact that I had told her the truth. Whether she believed it or not was of no consequence to me. I had told the truth, that's all that mattered. Right? Right?? Conveniently, this leads nicely into what happened next. Not her dying, but mentioning her.

Lost in thought, I'd just finished my coffee when my phone rang. I picked it up and looked at the caller ID. Shit. Her mother. What does SHE want?? She hadn't spoken to me since Helen had left. I was just staring at the phone ringing, wondering if I should answer. Why? *Well, why not? Do it.* But she hates me. *You don't know that.* It's obvious, isn't it? She thinks I cheated on her daughter.

But you didn't. Yeah, but I said so, remember? *Fuck.*

Hello?" I said hesitatingly into the phone.
"Jack, its Gloria, Helen's mum"
"Hi, Gloria" Wait, why the hell did she feel she had to tell me who she was, like I wouldn't know? Things were very weird.
"Helen was here and mentioned she had sent you a letter about picking up some stuff, but that you hadn't responded" Ah, so *that's* it. She realised I had no way to let her know, so got her *mother* to do her dirty work.
"Yes, but there was no return address, and she's blocked me on her phone, so I couldn't" I answered.
"Ah, yes. I see. Well, what can I tell her?"
"I have the kids tomorrow; I will take them out and leave a key with the neighbour; she can get it from her. I'll leave a list of items I want to keep" There was a moment of silence.
"She doesn't have a key?" she asked.
"No, I changed the locks after she left"
More silence. Then "I see". I detected a hint of anger in her voice. "Is that not a bit much?" She asked.
I took a breath, and a moment, then calmly said "Gloria, she left me. I don't want her and her new partner having access to my house. I'm not comfortable with that, as you can hopefully

understand. Tell her I'll be gone at 14.00, and home at 17.00."

If she did understand, she didn't say. She simply said "Well, I'll let her know. Bye Jack"

She was about to hang up, when I added "Gloria…."

Hesitation, then "Yes?"

"Can you please make sure she returns the key to the neighbour when she leaves?"

More silence, then "Yes" and she was gone. Shaking, I put the phone down.

Two things about the call that I was happy about:

1. I handled myself well, with confidence. I didn't let the situation intimidate me.

2. I made her mother aware that I knew that Helen had a new partner. Already.

Two things about the call that I was not happy about:

1. Her tone. She hated me, and it hurt.

2. I felt bad about the conversation. I had been quite short with her, and I still regret that.

After the call, I was angry.

With Helen. With Gloria. With myself.

After the call, I was worried.

Worried about what she would take from the house. Would it be empty when I got home?

I'd worry about that later. Right now, I had to go to work. Deadlines to be met. I lost myself in work till about 1900, when I shut my laptops down, picked up a pen & some post-its, sighed, and went downstairs.

I knew what I had to do, and it made me sad/angry/anxious. It brought it all home a bit more and seemed so clinical and final. But I went around putting notes on all the stuff I wanted to keep. Mostly stuff I had either bought or brought into the relationship. Then I went through the boxes of photographs we had and took out all pictures with her or her family in them and put them in a bag. I left it on the kitchen table, with a note that said, "Photographs for Helen". Then I just went around and anything that I found that was hers was put in bags. I just wanted all traces gone. No reminders required thanks. Three bags of random bits; makeup, cd's, dvd's, the odd bits of clothing.

Take them.

Bitch.

Difficult job. But I felt a bit better once I was finished. Like I had just cleared out all the badness in my life. It was almost midnight, and I needed sleep. Too late to eat, so I went to bed hungry. Sad about the days' events, but happy as I'd see my kids tomorrow.

Sherlock Holmes was about to crack a major mystery, but I missed it; I fell asleep almost immediately.

DAY 5

Wednesday, 5th of March.

A larm……ugh, too early. zzzzzzzzz……….. wakes up, checks clock; 08.12. Shit!!!!!! Kids coming today! Idiot in question jumps out of bed, showers quickly, and gets ready for the day. No run, he hasn't got time for that now. Dick.

Yeah, the day started badly; I was tired. Very tired. Physically, and emotionally. Even though the kids weren't coming till 11, I had a few work bits to finish up before they got here. No way was I going to finish everything I had to, so it was going to be a late night. But I didn't mind; my kids were more than worth it. My kids, mentioned them a few times, maybe I should tell you about them.

When I say "kids", they're 13 and 15…. I don't have to run around picking them up etc. They were old enough to catch the bus. I had no idea where they were living and didn't press the matter. She dropped them at her parents in Ramsey, and they got the bus from there. Right, so, the kids.

Boy, James, 15. Girl, Elsie, 13. They were everything I lived for. A parent's dream; no trouble, smart (WELL smarter than me), and very kind-hearted.

"How were they taking the divorce?" I hear you ask. Hmmm. Difficult to answer. Being teenagers, they were hard to read. They seemed ok, but you never know what is really going on in their heads. As far as the reason why, I was assured by Helen that she had told them we had simply drifted apart. I really hoped she had. I'd hate for my kids to think I was the cause. Because I wasn't. Do they? Well, let's see…. Jumping forward to the present time; they are fine. James away in Uni, Elsie doing A-Levels. Happy. And we have a great relationship.

Back to the story.

The kids would get here around 11, the bus leaving Ramsey at 10.50. I would take them out for a late lunch and walk around the shops in Peterborough. Bit of a treat, get them some new clothes, shoes, or whatever. That would give her time to go around the house and take her stuff. And then get out. Forever.

Wait. Hey, you; are you sure she won't go through all your drawers, check out your personal stuff? I had nothing to hide, but the thought filled me with anxiety. *What if she brought HIM. To YOUR house? What if HE went through your stuff?* Fuck. I hadn't thought about that. Thanks brain. I could only hope that she had the decency not to bring him, and really hoped she wouldn't.

……phone rings…….

Checks caller ID….her mother. *Again??*

"Hello?"

"Jack, I have spoken to Helen, and she will collect and drop off the key from the neighbour. She said she'd only need an hour or so." She said plainly. Not even a hint of emotion or friendliness.

"Oh, that's good. We'll be gone for a few hours anyway" I replied, trying to sound as casual as possible. Not sure how well I did, as I was feeling anything but casual.

"She's not overly happy about the locks being changed" She replied. WTF? Didn't we go through this earlier??

"Her happiness is no longer my concern I'm afraid." I responded, trying to mask the growing anger in my voice "Likewise, *my* house is no longer *her* concern" I added.

"Ok Jack." she sounded taken aback, but I didn't care.

"And tell her not to bring him. I don't want him in my house"

A pause. Then "Jack, she needs someone to help move her stuff. I'm sure it will be ok"

"Are you kidding? She's actually going to bring

him?" I asked angrily.

"Jack, I …" she began hesitantly. Before she could continue, I took a breath, and calmly replied.

"Forget about the key Gloria; her stuff will be on the driveway in bags"

"But…" she started, but I cut her off.

"Goodbye Gloria."

I hung up and threw my phone down on the sofa. I was soooo angry. Who the hell does she think she is? She's not happy about me changing the locks? Is she out of her fucking mind?? I went to the kitchen, and got a roll of bin bags, then started going around the house, bagging up anything that was obviously hers. When I had finished, there were 11 bin bags full of stuff. I didn't even care if she actually wanted all of it or not. I didn't care. I wanted it out of my house, and out of my life

I still had 30 minutes before the kids were due to arrive, so I put the bags on the drive, and quickly showered and changed.

It's hard to put into words how good it was to see my kids when they arrived. If you're not a parent, you couldn't imagine how much it hurts to be separated from your children. There is a tangent I can go off on here about crying myself to sleep, men's rights (non-existent), etc. But I'll save that for another chapter. In the meantime, I chose to forget about Helen, and have a good time with my lovely children. As we were reversing out of the drive, James asked "What's with the bags dad?"

Thoughts in my head where:

Should I tell them?
If I did, what would they say?
Would they take their mother's side?
Which side were they on?
Did they need to be on a particular side?

All of this took like a second or so in reality, and the thoughts were still scrolling through when I replied, "Just clearing out some old rubbish is all" It was the safest answer I could come up with on the spot. To my relief, Jack just said "cool" and started talking about school stuff. I'm not going to go into exactly what we got up to on that day, as it's both private, and irrelevant to this story. Needless to say, we had a great day, and it took my mind off the whole saga for a few hours. On the way back, I dropped them in Ramsey so they wouldn't have to get the bus. I hugged them fiercely and fought back the tears until they had gone into my in-law's house. I drove home sad. But also, happy. I was recharged; full of energy and feeling great.

Then I got home.

The bags were gone, so it was all over. Checked my phone; noting from Gloria. Just a few messages from clients. Still happy, I opened the front door and found an envelope.
I didn't need to open it to see who it was from; I recognised the handwriting.

Shit.

I was in too good a mood to let this get me down. I put the envelope on the kitchen table. How could I distract myself from it? Work. I grabbed a quick sandwich and went up to my lair.
Spent the rest of the evening working and managed to get all but 2 videos done. That means I have only 2 to complete tomorrow. Result. Checked watch: 00.37. Worth it. Got in bed and tried to lose myself in the wonderful Victorian world of Mr Holmes. Wasn't working. Fucking letter. Shit. Standby for another list....
Here's what kept going through my head:

What does she want?
Is it bad?
Will it be more legal stuff?
Is she angry?
Is it bad?
Is it bad?
Shit.

Couple of answers that could do with exploring here:

What does she want?
Emphasis on What. Does she want more stuff? Some of MY stuff? Stuff I hadn't thought of?

Is it bad?
I really just didn't want bad news right now. She could be going to town on me in writing. I wasn't

ready for that at the moment.

Will it be more legal stuff?
I thought we'd sorted everything out already. Is this something new? Or a new threat?

Is she angry?
Not that I would normally give a shit, but anger paves the way for revenge. She could shaft me for more money, access to the kids, etc. Didn't bare thinking about.

Try to put it out of your mind.

Try.

Nope, this shit is going to keep me awake all night.

Shit.

Bitch. (Obviously)

DAY 6

Thursday, 6th of March.

Alarm went off, but I was awake anyway. Sleep came sparingly last night. Fucking tired. My eyes are stinging. Running gear on, let's go. It was cold outside, and looked like it might even snow. Brrrrr. Went back in and got a hat. Setup watch, press start. The cold air hurt my throat as I ran along the tow path. Focus. Got to the halfway point, turned back. Few people out, not many. Frozen landscape, frosty, beautiful. Like a kid, I ran off the path to see how crunchy the grass was; very. Made me smile. Almost at the end of the path. Wait, is that Mary walking Chico? Yep, and for better or worse; she saw me coming.
"Morning Jack, isn't it lovely out?" she said brightly
I stopped and ended the run on my watch.
"Morning Mary. Yes, it's beautiful out here today"
The dog was sniffing me intently, obviously able to smell the cat on me.

"Chico! Down" she said, pulling the dog back.
"Don't worry, he just smells the cat is all" I offered in his defence.
"Ah, that would explain it" she laughed. "Sorry I can't stop; I have a bus to catch. Shopping day, come on Chico. Bye Jack, enjoy your day" And started walking off.
"No worries, have a nice day" I said, and gave the dog a quick goodbye stroke.
I checked my watch; not a bad time. Good effort Jack.
"Oh Jack…?"
I turned; Mary had stopped.
"Yes?" I replied, slightly puzzled.
"Your lace is undone." She waved and carried on walking.
Mood instantly moved up a few levels, just what I needed.

Got back, showered, made coffee, and lost myself in work. Although I only had two edits left, they were quite long videos. One was a review of a new line of guitars from a well-known manufacturer, the other an interview with an obscure folk musician that I had never heard of. Let's get to work Jack.

I finished the interview edit and sent it off to the client. Happy. Looked up at the roof window and saw that some snow was building up in the corners. Snow! I fucking loved snow! I had intended to just make a quick sandwich for my lunch but decided to go out instead. Yeah! Transferred the raw video to a laptop, put it in a bag, grabbed my coat, and left.

At this point, you're probably thinking "Open the fkn letter!" Yeah, part of me is asking exactly the same question. But……not doing that right now. Need to stay focussed for work. That could fuck up my day later on. With a beer or two.

My mate Steve (the one I helped move…) owned a small cafe near the canal, the "Cafe Jazz", so I made my way there. The snow was starting to stick, and the snowfall was getting heavier. This was going to be a good one! Happy, I walked into the café. The little bell tinkled as the door opened, and I heard Steve from behind the coffee machine "Fuck me sideways, look what the cat dragged in!" He emerged from a cloud of steam holding a cup. This guy has a way with words. Standby for increased use of bad language for a paragraph or so….. (Or for the rest of the book)
"Ello mate" I said. I found a table in the window and took off my coat.
"Are you fucking ill or something?" he asked, "Hardly ever see you here during the fucking week". (Told you)

"Well, I wasn't going to bother, as your coffee *is* shite, but it's freezing out, so I thought why the fuck not"

"Prick" he laughed. "Sit down, I'll get you a coffee." "Don't listen to him, my coffee is the fucking best" he said to a girl at the counter, handing her the drink he had just finished making. She just smiled and rolled her eyes at his language. She walked off with a smile. Smooth bastard. I looked around and saw that all 9 tables were taken. As usual at this time of day.

Wait. All taken? By whom? It's a small village, isn't it? Standby for another tangent….

Although Ramsey Forty Foot (stop laughing, get over it) was a small place, we had a few places of employment:

The Post office
The Shop
A Solicitors' Office
A Butcher
Steve's Cafe
The Pub
A Pet Grooming place

All the women in the café were from these various places, on their lunch break. Some even drove over from Ramsey. The ladies loved a bit of Steve; he was a cheeky lad. Tangent over. Just needed to expand on that, not sure why.

After a bit of hissing and a bit more swearing,

Steve walked over with my coffee. "You ok mate?" he put his hand on my shoulder.

"Yeah, think so bud" I said.

"Ok, just checking. You eating?" I got my laptop out and said

"Yep, you got anything edible?" "Cheeky bastard. I'll get you a ploughman's whilst you milk the free Wi-Fi for all its worth."

"Cheers man, appreciate it"

"Good to see you" He patted me on the back and walked back to behind the counter.

I flashed up the laptop, put on my headphones, and lost myself in video editing. I could hear the occasional bit of colourful language from Steve, and the resulting giggles from the ladies. They loved a bit of Steve. He brought over my lunch, which I ate whilst working. I really wanted to get this done today, I wanted tomorrow for myself. For some reason..... After a while, I looked up and noticed that the ladies had all gone, and Steve was just finishing cleaning the tables. He gave me a thumbs up, and I took my headphones off.

"Yeah, all good mate, about halfway through this vid. It's a big one" I saved my progress, and shutdown the laptop. He grabbed a couple of beers from the fridge and sat with me.

"Almost over now mate. To better times" we clinked bottles and took a sip. "How's it all going? Any new developments?"

I took another sip and told him about the calls

from Gloria and bagging up her stuff. He laughed "Fuck me mate, well done. I would have just chucked it out on the street"

"Yeah, well, can't really do that. As much as I hate her, I have to think of the kids." Steve was one of the few people that knew the truth behind the divorce, and he "fucking hated" her for it.

"So, she left me a letter" I said, letting it hang for a second.

"A fucking letter? You read it?"

"Nah, not yet"

"Why not you prick" he asked incredulously.

"Mate, I have work that needs finishing, and I knew if I read it, I'd get nothing done after".

"Good fucking point. You look after this pea sized thing in your head" poking at my head

I laughed. "Nice language mate"

"Ach, that's just me, take it or leave it. And believe me, the ladies take more than leave if you know what I mean" He winked.

"Eternal fucking bachelor" I said.

"Ha! Like it's an insult! Loving life bud, there's enough Steve for all the ladies."

"Big headed prick" I said.

"Absolutely. Now, pack your shit and get the fuck out. I'm closed" He laughed, stood, and grabbed his coat.

"Yeah, I'm done here anyways, the food is terrible, and don't even get me started on the service!"

"Fuck you man" he laughed. I put my coat on, and we stepped out into the snow.

After he finished locking up, he said "Pub. You, me. Soon. In the meantime, read the fucking letter and let me know what it says"
"Yes mate, I'll let you know".
"Fucking right you will!" he said.
We hugged and went our separate ways.

I walked home regretting not having gone to the toilet before stepping out into the cold. The coffee and beer needed to come out; my bladder was full. The snow was still falling, and it was getting pretty deep. What few cars I saw were driving very gingerly. The road gritter wouldn't come down from Ramsey till later tonight. After a couple of slippery incidents, I made it to the house. You want another quick tangent? I'll give you a quick one about the house.

My house. Never *our* house. We'd (I'd) bought the house after we'd been together for about 3 years. We were both from Ramsey, and it was quite rare for a young couple to stay local. Houses were cheaper over in the city, but we both loved village life. I was earning a great wage, so it wasn't hard to get a mortgage. We looked at a few places, in Ramsey, here in Forty Foot, and across the canal in Ramsey Mereside (where I worked). We both knew this was the one, even before we stepped foot inside. The location was great, it had a driveway, a garage, and a decent garden at the back. It's a 3-bedroom house, with a large kitchen, and the lounge has a conservatory. It was perfect.

It was cheaper than we would expect, which was suspicious.

"It's a great place" I told the estate agent showing us around "But what's with the price?"

"Ah, yes, there is an issue with the property" she said, "And I'm not going to lie to you Jack, it'll cost a bit to put right" We had known Jane for years, we had gone to school together.

"What is the issue?" I asked.

She pointed up "The thatch roof. It needs replacing" She cringed as she said it.

I whistled "That's not cheap".

"No, but its ok guys, I have a few more places to show you" she said apologetically. I looked at Helen "It's not that bad, I can get it done" I assured her. She nodded. "Jane, its ok, I think we're home. We'll take it"

She looked worried "Are you sure guys? I mean, I have other places to show you"

"You're a terrible salesperson Jane" I laughed "Don't worry about the roof. We'll take it".

We went from there really. I had the roof done and got a good price from my Uncle Brian's mate. We had a smell loft conversion done at the same time, so it took a while to finish. But it was stunning. The canal runs behind the house, separated from the house by a small, wooded area. It's south facing, so the garden does really well. We planted rosemary, lots of lavender, and a few fruit trees. It looks and smells fantastic in the summer. Our neighbour 4 doors down has bees, and they are all over the garden when the plants blossom. It's truly idyllic. Hence, I *had* to find the money to buy her out. There was no way I was losing this house.

Back to the story…

I got in & went straight to the loo. I was bursting. I put the kettle on for a cup of tea and sat at the table. Staring at the letter. "I should open it" I thought. *No, you idiot. Get a cup of tea and finish your work.* Yes, good call brain. I made the tea and went upstairs. I transferred the file from my laptop and spent the next 4 hours finishing it. I was exhausted. I clicked send and shut down the pc.

It was 22.03. Work done, free day tomorrow. That means I can stay up and have a few beers. I got a beer from the fridge, picked up the letter and went into the lounge. I put some music on and sat on the sofa. Immediately, the cat appeared from nowhere, and jumped up on my lap. She curled up and closed her eyes. My eyes, meanwhile, were on the letter in my hand. "Jack" it said on the front. I took a breath and opened it. Inside was a single folded sheet of paper.

I opened it up, and looked at the first words "My dearest Jack" What the fuck? My dearest Jack? This from the woman that had blocked me out of her life completely, and only spoke to me through a solicitor or her mother. My dearest Jack. Jesus.

Fuck. Shit. I could give you a list of thoughts that were going through my mind, but I'll spare you, and instead just present you with the letter:

My dearest Jack,

I hope this letter finds you well. I really mean that. I know these times have been difficult, particularly for you. For this I am truly sorry. You should know that I have told the kids the truth about the reason for the divorce. I owed you that much at least. Rest assured, I will never stop them from seeing you, they are free to do so whenever they desire. I am really sorry about all the legal dealings and blocking you from my phone. I have my reasons, which I won't go into.

Thank you for returning my belongings, and the extra photographs. I am grateful. It was difficult coming here, as so many memories came rushing back to me, making it all very emotional. There is nothing more I want from the house, so please rest easy on that front. I was a bit taken aback when I heard you had changed the locks, but on reflection, it's only logical. I should thank you for leaving my stuff outside, as I wasn't looking forward to entering the house.

You should also know that I came with my Dad. I know you would have been worrying about that; I wouldn't have done that to you.

I hope you find it in your heart to eventually forgive me, and I hope that you once again find love in your life. You deserve that so very much.

Take care Jack, and thank you for so many wonderful memories that will stay in my heart forever.

Helen.

I read it 4, 5, 6 times. What the hell was going on here? Just what the actual fuck was going on? I was genuinely puzzled. This was not the person I had been dealing with recently. This was not the content I was expecting. This was not supposed to be happening. Why was she being nice? Why was she showing such remorse? This was all her idea, her doing. She had no right to show remorse.

This letter could have had two impacts:

1. It could make me angry. It *should* make me angry. How the hell dare she, after all she's put me through over the last 8 months. She had no right to show remorse, or to be sorry, or to wish me well. She lost all of those rights when she signed the divorce paper. Fuck. This made me bitter and hate her even more. Bitch.

2. It could put my mind at ease. She had told the

kids the truth. It didn't matter to me what anyone else in the universe knew, as long as my kids knew the truth. I would hate for my kids to disown me or think badly of me. She had ensured that wouldn't happen. I was grateful. I was relieved. I was happy. Yes, happy.

So, what do you reckon? How would you have felt in my place? Angry? Happy? Think about it. Both options make sense, but it all depends on what kind of person you are.

Spoiler alert; I went for option 2.

This letter took so much weight off my mind, I felt like I was floating. My kids knew the truth. She didn't want anything else from the house. She was genuinely sorry about all the stress and anguish she had caused. I believed her. I knew her well enough to know she was being genuine.

So, yes, thank you Helen. For that one thing, I thank you. For the rest; fuck you.

I put the letter back in the envelope and put it through the shredder in my office room. Nobody ever needed to see that again. I didn't for sure.

I was tired. Very tired. Mentally and physically. It was hard work, trying to stay positive. Or putting on a positive front at least. It was all for show. Inside, I was slowly dying. Heading for a fall. It would come. When, I didn't know. I just knew it would.

Despite all the things going around my head, sleep came easy; no need for Mr Holmes tonight.

DAY 7

Friday, 7th of March.

Before I continue the story, I should probably go off on a rather important tangent; how we came to the point of divorce.

Sigh. I should really have seen it coming. The changes in affection (lack of), increased nights out without me, and the subsequent very late returns home. She was in the gym 5 nights a week and seemed obsessed with fitness. She was distant, spent a lot of time on her phone, and she'd started smoking (goes against the fitness thing I know). All these changes should have caused alarm bells to ring, but they honestly didn't. I was worried and suspicious of course, but not to the point that I would end our marriage. As it happened, she did that for me. After a few weeks of this, she asked me to sit with her in the lounge. She sat in a chair, in the corner of the room. After all this time, I can still see her there in my mind. I know exactly what she was wearing, how her hair was. How featureless her face was. How utterly horrible she was in that moment.

I asked what was up, and she responded. Very calmly, very coldly.

"I should tell you that I have filed for divorce. You should be receiving papers to sign in a few days. It's not working anymore, and it's for the best" With these 30 words, she destroyed my life. If she saw the effect of her words, she didn't let it show. She was cold, and clinical.

"I would like to stay here in the house until I have found somewhere to live. I will move into the spare bedroom." I was destroyed. I didn't know what to say. I just sat there and cried. She got up and went upstairs to move her stuff out of the bedroom. I just sat there, in silence, crying. What the hell just happened? How was this happening to me?

Looking at it from the outside, you would think I would have argued with her, asked if there was someone else, asked why I wasn't good enough, asked how she could do this to our family. I just couldn't. I was just completely fucked. My head wasn't working.

It wasn't until the following afternoon that I asked all these questions. The kids were in school, and I came home in my lunchtime to ask. Yes, there was someone else, he worked at the gym (Shock...). I asked why she wasn't moving in with him. She said his place was too small. Too small? Yes, too small for me and the kids. Wait. The kids? You're taking the kids?? Of course, they're coming with me. No, they're fucking not. They are, the divorce papers will say so, and it's all been arranged. Arranged? When? What? Slowly, I was losing my grip on reality. She was taking my kids away from me. I felt myself spiralling towards rock bottom. I went to my room and crashed. Mentally, and physically. I cried for hours. I was dead inside.

You can guess where this is going next. Standby for a Father's Rights rant.

According to the law, the children go to the mother by default. It is then left to the father to fight to see his children, or to somehow prove that the mother is unfit. It's pathetic. It's like Father's have no feelings, or never want to have anything to do with their kids. My kids are my life. I live for them. Everything I do is for them. I can't imagine life without them. (And I didn't) This means nothing to the British legal system. Absolutely nothing.

So many dads out there end up taking their own lives as they can't imagine a future without their children. Nobody seems (seemed) to care. I was at the mercy of whatever scraps of access she was willing to throw my way.

Also, I find it amazing that most people automatically take the woman's side in a divorce. It's shocking. It's like females are incapable of wrongdoings. It's always the man's fault. Misinformation often plays a role here. Most only ever hear one side of a story. This is particularly difficult if you live in a small community. You're treated like an outcast. People ignore you in the streets, people you thought were friends suddenly disappear out of your life. It all adds to the anguish felt by millions of us out there. Even people you know will sometimes joke "Ooh, been caught out have eh mate?" There's this auto-assumption that you are the cause. It's pathetic. And most times you're too drained to defend yourself.

I guess its times like those that you find out who your real friends are. The genuine ones. I certainly did. Steve was the first, and only, friend to text me to see how I was. I don't even know how he knew as I hadn't told him. But there he was; ready to support his friend. When you find people like Steve, keep them close forever. They'll be there for you, no matter what. And, trust me, you'll need them. Ah, also, I'd just shredded the letter. Why would I want to do that?? I had spells of regret afterwards, but it was for the best. A kind of closure if you like.

Anyhoo, let's get on with Friday.

No alarm today, I woke at 08.12 after a good night sleep. As per usual, my day was going to start with a run. I opened the curtains, and there was at least a foot and a half of snow. Negative on the outdoor run. Good thing I have a treadmill for such occasions! I got changed and did 5k on the treadmill. Not my preferred option I must add. I prefer being out in the open air, it was just better.

Shower, dress. Coffee & cinnamon bagels. Radio was telling me that the weather wasn't going to get any better, and there would be nationwide rail and road closures etc. Typical UK I thought, never prepared for anything. But…. wait…. rail strikes…. Would Chrissy be able to get here with the trains out and roads closed? *Why did that come to mind? You barely know her. Why would you think of her?* Well, let's face it; she made a hell of an impression on me. Those brief encounters had really affected me. It had been so long since I had been in female company, apart from family of course. Since I kicked Helen out, there had been nobody. Wait? What? You kicked her out?? Worthy of a minor tangent…

You'll recall she wanted to stay in the house until she found somewhere to live? Yeah, so that went on for 3 weeks. The atmosphere in the house was terrible, and I found myself spending more and more time out of the house. In the end, the school summer holiday had started, so I decided now was the right time to take action. I told her I wanted her out immediately, because this wasn't going well. But I have nowhere to go! You can go live with your parents; they have the space. You can look for somewhere else from there. This was out of character for me, but I was at my wits' end. She had to go. Heartless? Kicking my kids out? They would be just fine, and they loved their grandparents. I needed her gone. Or it wouldn't end well. She protested more, but I told her I wanted her gone before I came home from work the following day. She cried, and created a bit of a drama, but she did it. I came home the next day, and she was gone. I'd never felt so relieved in my life. I could breathe.

Road closures. Shit. Would that mean I wouldn't see her? (Yeah, we're back into the story) I text Steve to see if he was opening up today. He responded a few minutes later, saying he was already on his way. I had no plans, so I asked if he needed help. I did that sometimes; it was great fun. Sure! He said. Always welcome. We could have a laugh. And you can tell me about the letter……

Ah yeah. Shit. The letter. But, I thought, there's nothing to worry about. The letter was all good. Interested to see how Steve would react though. 1 or 2?

"Fucking bitch" Yeah, deffo a 2…. Steve was busy baking the morning pastries, and I had just finished reading out the letter to him from memory.
"Mate, it's all good. I'm ok with it" I replied, trying to make him see that it was really ok.
"But dude, she's full of shit. After all that shite she put you through, she's suddenly being fucking nice??" I just shrugged.
"Nah, I'm not fucking buying it. But it's up to you"

"Yeah, I guess it is. And I'm really ok with it mate"
He thought for a second, then "Well if you are, then who the fuck am I not to be eh"
We hugged. "Still a bitch though" he said. The man wasn't wrong she really was a bitch, but...
"Oh, fuck yeah" I said.
"Can't believe you shredded it though"
"Hmmmm, yeah. It was for the best. It was like closure. Don't need to ever read it again"
He looked at the trays of pastries, nodded, and then said "Fair enough. Right, let's get cracking." He threw me an apron, and I started setting up the coffee machine. I was still thinking that he wasn't wrong; she had been a complete bitch so far. Why was she now suddenly being all nice? *Wait. Don't let this consume your day. Put it out of your mind. Now Jack!* As it happened, I wouldn't have time to think about it anyway. Shit was about to get real.

The machine beeped a few times, indicating it was warmed up and ready to go. "Ok mate, go" I called over to Steve. He walked over and flipped the sign on the door to "open". He looked at me and nodded, as if to say, "You ready for this??" I gave him the thumbs up. I was ready. Ready for some distraction. This was going to be tough; it was going to get...The little bell tinkled before I could finish my thought. Here they come. I took a deep breath, and completely lost myself in the morning rush.

"Jesus mate, how do you manage that all by yourself?" I asked as I dropped down into a chair. The morning rush had subsided; we had survived. It was only 09.10, and I was shattered.

"Piece of piss mate. You form a routine, and it's fucking easy after that." He said with a smirk.
"Bullshit. You need help. This will end up killing you."
"Nah, it's all good"
"No, it isn't dickhead, get some help"
"You reckon?"
"Yes, I do. Sort it. Today"
"Ok mate, I'll get an advert out tonight."
"Good. Not like you can't afford it"
He perked up "Yeah, you're right there. I make enough in the morning; I don't really need to be open in the afternoon. It's all just extra money."
"There you go" I said with a smile. "I'm fucked, don't know how you do this day after day".
"Ach, you think *that* was busy? Wait till lunchtime matey, that's pure hell!" Something to look forward to.... Whilst Steve busied himself with pastries, sandwiches, and rolls, I cleaned tables, filled the dishwasher, and cleaned the coffee machine. 20 Minutes later, we were stood at the counter, our work done.

"Fuck me, let's have a sit down" I said.
Steve laughed. "You grab a seat, and I'll grab us a coffee and some pastries." We sat in the window, feeling grateful for the quiet, and food. The pastries were fantastic. The company was great. The coffee was genius. (Obviously). Life was good. Yeah, in that little moment; life was good.

I looked out the window. Outside, the snow had

started to fall again, and I was roused from my bliss with a sudden thought.

"You think they'll close the roads?" I asked.

"Oh, fuck yeah, look at it." I stared out into the snow, and just thought "Fuck". Didn't bare thinking about. *Put it out of your mind Jack.*

Behind me, the bell tinkled. Rush hour done, it was time for the old ladies to come and have coffee and catch up on the latest gossip. There were quite a few of them eventually, but it was all at a more relaxed pace.

"Morning ladies, looking beautiful as ever" Steve offered our guests with a big smile and open arms. They giggled and formed an orderly queue. Smooth bastard.

The rest of the morning and early afternoon was a blur of coffee, sandwiches, and more coffee. Faces came and went, familiar, yet strangers all the same. Steve seemed to know them all, he was extremely good at this. It was 14.23, and I was officially fucked. So tired…. Steve had gone off to the wholesaler in Ramsey, and I had sat in the window with a sandwich. I hadn't thought about the divorce all day, but now that I had a moment of silence, the thoughts came creeping back. Not in a bad way I guess, just me going over the facts in my head.

It was all done. Set in stone. Regardless of whether I agreed with everything. It was done. Being angry or bitter about it wasn't going to change anything. I had been there, and then some. I found myself at home shouting really loudly, just to get the frustration out. You ever seen the movie "Dead Poet's Society"? "Let out a barbaric yelp" That's what I did. And it made me feel better. Not sure what the neighbours thought. It is a detached home, but still, it's a quiet village right....

Eventually though, it was all ok. I had reached the point of acceptance.

It had taken me a while to get here, and I still faltered occasionally, but I had accepted that this was all real. Best place to be. Trust me.

Acceptance. Interesting. Let's talk about that for a second (tangent). Humour me, it's a very important part of the book.

If you weren't aware, there are 5 distinct stages of grief. These stages can be applied to other circumstances than grief. Divorce for example.

The stages are, in order:

- Denial.
- Anger.
- Bargaining.
- Depression.
- Acceptance.

Have a look, then think of a bad situation you've experienced in your life. Then look at the stages again and you'll see that it's not an unfamiliar process to you. They're familiar right? Here's how they applied to me during this divorce:

- Denial.

Remember what she said? "I should tell you that I have filed for divorce.... blah blah...

it's not working…blah" How did Denial come into this for me? Let's look at some thoughts/comments:

- What? It is working.
- There's nothing wrong with our marriage.
- She's kidding.
- It's not serious
- It'll never happen.
- She'll change her mind.

You are basically stupefied. Surely things aren't *that* bad? You know they are, of course, but don't want to admit to it. Once you realise it IS real, you get to….

- Anger.

Bitch. Not sure that ever goes away completely (that's me speaking from the future!). Sure, you forget eventually. But, once in a while, you remember. And get angry again. Even if it is just for a second. Thoughts:

- How dare she do this to me?
- Bitch
- You're taking MY kids away from ME?
- Bitch
- I hate you
- Bitch
- Etc.
- Etc.

Oh, my life, I was angry. Fuck her. Who the hell does she think she is, taking my kids away?? (Think back to my dad's rights rant...) Bitch. Eventually, you get over it. Not completely, and not forever. You still have a bit of anger but start thinking you can probably sort something out. Surely. Leading to....

- Bargaining.

Shit. It's real. I was pissed off, but now.... I don't want this to happen. I can reason with her right? Please don't do this to me. Please. Maybe if I could just talk to you about it? We can make this work, surely? I'll be better. Tell me what to do to make it better?? (Even though it's not my fault). You try to reason with her. Try to convince her that all this isn't necessary, that you can work it out. But you get nowhere. So, then you get to.......

- Depression.

Alarm bells. Pay attention. This is a HARD stage to get through. Make sure you have support. Make sure you have loved ones that check on you. You hit rock bottom. Ground zero. All sorts of thoughts go through your head, jostling for attention:

- I'm useless.
- I can't make her happy.
- I'm useless.
- I've failed my kids.
- I'm really useless.

- I want to be with my kids.
- I'm more than useless.
- I NEED to be with my kids.
- I'm totally, utterly useless.
- I can't live without my kids.
- I don't want to live.
- Nobody will miss me.
- I want to die.

Look at the last 4. Please, look at them. That's where you're likely to get to, and then you start getting stupid; you try to kill yourself. Nah, won't happen to me, I'm fine. Think again. Look it up; 4 in 10 men consider suicide after divorce. It's all out there, read up on it. 4 in 10. Most likely the 4 out of the 10 where kids are involved, and the dad is fully engaged in their lives. There are dad's that don't really care & abandon their kids; the worst kind of human being. You have kids? You love them more than anything? You're one of the 4 in 10.

I'm here to say; don't. I tried it but failed. Thankfully. And I mean thankfully. Here's why:

- YOUR KIDS.

In capitals. Because it's true. Why do that to your kids? You think they'll think better of you because you sacrificed yourself? Don't be an idiot. Think again. They will have to live with the stigma for the rest of their lives. Instead of making it better, you make it worse. Sure, you made your ex feel terrible, but in the process, you fucked up your kids' lives. Moron.

When I failed (I won't go into it), I realised that I needed to be there for my kids. I needed to be alive, needed to get through this. Divorce=bad, limited access=bad, finances=bad. But death? Think about it. Please, just do. Things may look bad, and there's no way out. But it's just superficial, and deceptive. I was there, I tried the easy way out. I failed. And I'm eternally grateful that I'm still here. It does get better. IT DOES. No bullshit. You can live with limited access, because you STILL see your kids. Divorce? Hah. Fuck her. She's gone. Finances? You'll make do. Being alive is better than being dead. Seeing your kids grow up, giving them random hugs, giving them all the love and support they need to survive in life. You can't do that from beyond the grave. Don't do it. Please.

I'm not going to lie; I still get mini spells of depression. But you WILL eventually get to….

- Acceptance.

This is the most important stage. You HAVE to accept that nothing you do or say is going to change anything. ACCEPT. And move on. (-ish) Look, you reach a certain level of acceptance. Not like "Accepted! I'm happy now" but accepted enough to move on with your life. There will be relapses, but minor, and fewer as time goes on. Be proud of yourself. Here's what you've achieved:

- You got through stages; 1, 2, 3.
- You got through the worst stage; 4. Really, be proud you got through that.

- You've become the bigger person in the divorce.
- Your ex will be reeling, expecting you to have crashed.
- Your kids still have you.
- You still have you kids.
- You've proven you can meet adversity head-on. And win.
- You'll be a stronger person.
- You can move on with your life.
- You're alive.

Saved the best till last. You're alive. None of this is any good if you aren't. Remember that.

Well done. You should be really proud of yourself.

Erm, where were we? Ah, Steve was out, and I'd reached acceptance. I was quietly chuffed with myself for getting there. I got up and took my plate out to the sink to wash. As I was doing that, the bell tinkled. "Be right there, just a sec" I shouted. "No rush" was the response. I nearly dropped my plate. I recognised the voice instantly. I dried my hands and walked out to the counter. There she was. Beautiful. Radiant smile.

"Hi" I just about managed.

"Hi, I hear this is the place to come for a good coffee"

"Yes, it is. I mean, we do coffee. Good coffee." She laughed at my awkwardness

"A cappuccino then please".

"Yes, of course"

"Ooh and one of those please" She pointed at a cinnamon swirl.
"Good choice, my favourite." I said. More smiles. "Please have a seat, I'll bring it over" She walked off, and I noticed she sat in the chair I usually sat in; in the corner, by the window. Making the coffee, I had a quiet word with myself. "Get yourself together Jack!"

I finished making the coffee and took the drink and pastry over. "Finest coffee, and delicious pastry" I said as I put them on the table.
"Looks delicious" she said. "Chrissy, by the way" she said and held out her hand.
I shook it and responded "Yes, I know. Jack, by the way" We were shaking hands. God, her hand was so warm and soft....
"Yes, I know" she said with a smile. "You can let go now"
"Oh, sorry, yes, of course." I let go of her hand (reluctantly). "I met your aunt the other day" I offered
"Yes, she said. She said you were very nice." Smile.
"She's lovely" I replied.
"Yes, she is. Sit with me?" she said before I could manage anything else.
"Yes, sure" I pulled out a chair and sat down. What was wrong with me? I felt like an awkward teenager. *Fuck's sake Jack, sort yourself out.* I was furiously trying to think of something to say.
She saved me. "Tell me a bit about yourself Jack. Are you a local boy?"
"Me? Erm, yes, born and raised here."
She looked at my hand, and said "Does your wife

mind you talking to other women?" I blushed, hard. Wow.

"I am divorced. Well, close to. Almost. You know, in the process of getting divorced" Awkward.

"Ah, I see".

"Apologies, feeling a bit awkward" I said.

She laughed, then "I hadn't noticed. Do you mind talking about it?"

"About what?"

"The divorce".

"Ah, no, not really. It is what it is. It's been dragging on for 8-9 months now, but almost over."

"Eight months, that must be difficult for you?"

"Yes, it's not been easy for sure" then I quickly added "The divorce, it's not my fault."

"I wasn't going to ask" She responded.

"Yes, but I know everybody wonders. I just wanted you to know it wasn't my fault."

"Ok, thank you."

Jesus, what are you doing Jack????

The bell tinkled again; Steve had returned from the wholesalers.

"Gimme a hand here mate would you, its fucking heavy"

"Won't be a moment" I said to Chrissy, then jumped up and went out to help bring the supplies in. "Who's the bird? And don't tell me she's a customer"

"She's a friend" I responded.

"A friend, eh?" wink wink….

"Just a friend Steve."

"Whatever you say matey. Whatever you say". We finished storing all the stuff out the back, and I went back to the counter.

She was gone.

Shit.

Fuck.

I was dejected.

Steve cleared the table and walked over.

"Your "friend" left you a note" he said handing me a small piece of paper. I took it, and the theatrical winks and elbow nudges from Steve.

"Funny. See you later" I grabbed my coat and was out the door before he could respond.

He ran after me, and I heard him shout from the door "Mate, we still good for a pint later?"

I didn't look back, just stuck my finger up at him.

"I'll take that as a maybe. Let me know you prick!"

I turned the corner and stopped. The note. I took it out. My name was on it. Nice handwriting. I unfolded it and read.

Jack,

Sorry, had to dash. Call or message me, and we'll try again.

C.

07211402835.

Her number. I have her number. This was a big step, right? Right? I felt like I'd just won the lottery or something. With a spring in my step, I made my way home. Very happy.

Having her number presented me with a whole new set of problems. Well, problems for me at least. Thoughts:

- When do I text/call? (don't want to seem too keen/desperate)
- What do I say? I needed time to think about it.
- Should I call/text her at all?
- What would the kids think?
- Is it too soon? (don't want to fall into the "Rebound" trap)

Me being me, I looked online to see what it said about how soon is too soon. Depends on the person. Making sure your heart & head are in the same place. To me, they were. It felt like I remember; falling in love.

Watched a few episodes of 24, ordered pizza in (yes, there's a pizza place in Ramsey....), had a few beers. Went through my messages; Mum checking up on me, clients all happy with their videos (thankfully), and Steve wanting to go out tomorrow.

Keeping it short, as this has been a long chapter already!

Should I text? Hmmmm.

In the end, I decided to sleep on it. Maybe I'd be in a better position to make a decent decision tomorrow. As Mr Holmes would say "This is a three-pipe problem Watson". Speaking of which, headphones in, I have an appointment at 221b.......

One final thought:

Thank you, Ramsey Town Council, for clearing the

roads.

DAY 8

Saturday, 8th of March.

Woke early this morning. No alarm set, just my body used to the routing of getting up early. 06.20. FFS. Ah, look. There it is, on the bedside table. The note. I picked it up, got my phone, and created a new contact. Too early to text now. Leave it till later. What you going to say though? I could suggest meeting at the café, but I'd rather not as Steve would just give me grief. Pub? Too soon? A walk maybe? Seemed like a safer option. A walk it is. Along the canal. She could bring the dog. Not a dog fan, but in this case…. Decision made. Get up.

Opened curtains, still snow everywhere. Nice. It looked very pretty outside; I loved the snow. Not great running weather but would be awesome for a walk. Yeah.

Full of happiness, I got changed, and did my 5k on

the treadmill. Shower, change, breakfast. No, wait. No breakfast. I felt bad about walking away from Steve. Breakfast at his it is.

Tinkle….

"Hey man"

Steve looked up and smiled "Morning bud".

"Sorry about yesterday mate" I said.

"Ach, leave it. It's all good man. I should be sorry, should be more careful. I know you're in a bad place."

I went behind the counter and hugged my friend.

"Love you man".

"You too dickhead. You eating?"

"Fuck yeah" I said

"Sit, I'll sort you out".

I went and sat in my usual table and stared out of the window. Like to say I was people watching, but in a village this small, that was at a premium. Although, there was someone making their way towards the café. It was usually pretty quiet at the weekend, and I didn't really understand why Steve didn't just close. He said the village needed somewhere to go, as there was nowhere else. And besides, he got on average about 20 customers a day at the weekend, so it was ok. He got the opportunity to sit and do his admin in between, so even better.

"Here you go champ, get that down ya!" He put down a plate with my usual pastry, and a sausage Bap.

"Sausage baps now?" I asked.

"Expansion matey, only at the weekend though. Sausage and bacon only. Nothing fancy"

"Nice move dude. When word gets out, they'll be queueing out the door".

"That's the idea man. And…. I put out a job advert last night. I have my first interview in an hour." He smiled proudly.

"Good effort, you'll need it after news of these gets out" I said, nodding at the sausage Bap.

"Enjoy mate" He patted me on the back and went back to the counter to serve the guy that was about to walk in. the door opened, and a gust of cold air hit me. Brrrr! Jesus it was cold outside. I sipped my coffee, then tucked into my breakfast.

I was sat with my second cappuccino, when the door opened, and a girl (lady, woman; you choose. think mid-30s or so) walked in. She stood at the counter, looking nervous. Steve came out from the kitchen and greeted her warmly. "Hi, I'm here for the interview?" She said quietly.

"Of course. Come, let's sit at the table there." He came out, and they both sat at a table.

"Jack, would you mind?" he asked, nodding at the counter.

"Sure mate, no prob." I got up and asked the girl if she'd like a drink.

"Latte please, if that's ok?" she turned quickly to check with Steve.

"Of course, it is" he smiled. I went off and made the

girl her drink.
"Thank you"
"You're welcome" I smiled. I went out into the kitchen, to be out of the way. If a customer came, I'd go out and serve. In the meantime, I had a text to send.

Took me about 10 minutes to word the text, but I did it, and sent it. Sent. Relief. And…. breathe. Spent a while faffing around on my phone, giving Steve privacy. No customers came in the 30 minutes he took to interview the girl. I heard them get up and I walked back out to the counter. Steve was just showing her out the door "Thanks Willow, see you tomorrow" He closed the door, and turned with a happy look on his face "Done!" he said.
"Done? One interview?" I asked incredulously.
"Mate, she's worked at a Costa in PB, so is fully fucking trained already. I'd be stupid not to take her, right?"
"Fair point. Worked out well then"
"Yes mate, happy days. Thanks for pushing me."
"Welcome".
"Now then, who's this mysterious bird?" We sat, and I told him all about it.
(*PB = Peterborough in Steve speak)

I left Steve at 10.30; still no reply. Slightly disappointed, I decided to go and see my parents. My mum was worried, and I hadn't seen them for a week. For info, they're over the canal in Ramsey

Mereside. I walked over the bridge, and saw, in the distance, a figure walking a dog along the tow path. Could it be? *Nah, just go to your parents.* I did. Mum was over the moon, and very fussy. I had to tell her three times that yes, I have had breakfast. Dad told her to stop fussing. She made tea, and we sat and chatted. We went through the usual, how I was, if I was eating ok, how the kids were, how work was, and how things were going with the divorce. Standard parent visit stuff. An hour later, I hugged my parent's goodbye, and walked out with a bag containing scones, and a piece of lemon meringue. Good old mum, love her dearly.

I walked back home, didn't see Chrissy about anywhere on the way. Mildly disappointed, I lit the fire in the lounge, and parked myself on the sofa with the tv remote. Confession time; I love black and white movies. I flicked through, and found a movie called Man on the Run, genius. An hour later, just as Jean had found the man with the missing fingers in the café, my phone binged. I picked it up and saw that it was from Chrissy. Fuck! Unlock, open message. She'd love to go for a walk, would I be free at 1600? Didn't even need to think about it; yes. Text back straight away. A sense of excitement filled me, for the first time in a long time. Bing! Open message. Meet you by the bridge at 1600. X. Excellent. It was 13.27 now, so I had ages to get ready. Shower and a change of clothes. Didn't really need it but wanted to make a good impression. *Wait. Wait. Wait. An X?* Is that just something women did naturally? No, hang on, it wasn't on the other message, just this one. *A good sign?* I hoped so. I watched the rest of the movie in a daze; I'm sure they caught the two guys in the end though.

After a shower, change, and several mirror checks, I made my way to the bridge. I was early. Very early. It was only 15.40, and she was nowhere to be seen when I got there. Idiot. Why did you leave so early?? It was too cold to be stood still, so I walked around for a bit to keep warm. Just before 4, I saw Chrissy walking up to the bridge. I was just making my way towards there and waved. She waved back and waited for me to get there.

"Hi" I said as I walked up. The dog was happy to see me, or to smell the cat. Either way, it seemed a good thing.

"Hi! How are you? You look cold!"

"Yeah, I may have been a bit early, so went for a wander" The dog was still sniffing me, its tail wagging

"Ah. You want to get moving then, get warm? Chico seems to have taken to you." she observed

"Yeah, we've met a few times now haven't we boy?" I gave the dog a stroke, and we started walking.

"You're not a dog person, are you?" she said laughing.

"To be honest, no. Never have been." I admitted. Shit. How would that go down?

"I can tell. It's ok though, don't worry". Pfew. I was trying to think of something to say. *Anything!*
"How is you aunt?" I asked. *Is that it? The best you had??* Do one, inner voice!
"Oh, she's fine thanks. Not a fan of the cold weather, but she's surviving"
"Good. I mean, good that she's ok. The weather is here to stay for another 2 weeks or so according to the weatherman this morning." *What? Why are you talking about the weather now?*
"Shame, I wouldn't want to get stuck here" she replied
"No, of course not" I said, mildly concerned.
Must have been written on my face, because she quickly added "I was kidding. I love this place, it's so quiet."
"Yeah, quiet for sure."
"I like quiet. You ever lived in the city?" she asked
"No, never. Not my scene I'm afraid. I'm a village boy to the core."
"I can see why" she said, whilst looking out the scenery "Look at it, it's beautiful"
"It's good enough for me" I said, proudly
"I can see why you wouldn't want to leave" she said with a sigh
"Something wrong?"
"I'm getting tired of city life, and coming here to see my aunt has made it worse"
"Not many jobs going around here if you were looking to move" I said cautiously. *Was she looking to move here?* That would be great, obviously. But,

play it cool Jack.
"Oh, I'm based at home anyway, so I could theoretically live anywhere" *Yes! Result!*
"As long as there was good internet of course" she added questioningly
"Well, I work out of a home office, and the internet here is great. We live close enough to the city to have fibre"
"Ooh, that's good" she smiled.
The dog started dragging her off towards a bush, obviously haven smelled something interesting.
"Chico!" she laughed and stumbled after the dog. The snow was deeper, and she was struggling a bit. I ran after her and offered to take the dog.
"Thanks, I can't stop him once he gets the smell of something" she explained.
"It's cool, I've got him". I took the lead and started to pull the dog back towards the path. Reluctantly, Chico gave up, and followed.
She was stood on the path, stamping her feet to get the snow off her boots and jeans.
"Oh, I'm freezing now! Thanks Chico" There was still humour there, but it was starting to wane.
"How about a hot chocolate?" I offered
"Yes please" she said thankful
"I know just the place" I said.
We started walking back towards the village, and she asked if we could drop the dog back home before the drink.
"Sure, it's just around the corner" It's not really, but in a small village, *everything* is "just around the

corner". We left the dog with Mary and made our way to Steve's cafe.

"You spend a lot of time there?" she asked, nodding towards the cafe down the street.

"Steve is my best mate. We've known each other since birth. So yeah, I do. I like to help out when I have time off"

"It gets busy?

"Oh yeah. Breakfast and lunch times, it's rammed."

"And he does all that alone?" she asked incredulously

"Used to. He just hired a girl to help out"

I walked in, and held the door open for her. There were a few people sat around, and my usual table was taken. We opted for the only other available table, close to the counter.

"Hot chocolate?" I asked

"Ooh yes please" she said, trying to rub some warmth into her hands.

"Ello matey" Steve gave me a smile and a wink. "You good?"

"Yes mate, all good." smile.

"What can I get you?"

"Two hot chocolates please"

"You want all that shite on top?" he asked. I rolled my eyes and said yes.

He went off to start making the drinks, and I dropped a 20-pound note in his tip jar. He never charged me for anything, so I usually put a sneaky £20 in his tip pot when he wasn't looking.

He knew, but never said anything.

I went back and sat down. "He'll bring them over in a mo" I said to Chrissy.

"This seems like a nice place, and he seems like a nice guy. He obviously cares about you; he hasn't stopped peeking over from behind the machine since you came back." She smiled

"Oh really?" I said in a deliberate raised voice as I turned around. I just caught Steve ducking away.

She giggled. "He's funny"

"Yeah, he's funny alright"

"Bless him, it's good to have someone that's looking out for you"

"He sure does that. But I like to think we look out for each other."

She took a sip of her drink "Ooooh that's good"

"Best barista in the village" I said, quickly adding "Only barista in the village"

She laughed. That's a good thing, I thought to myself. I'm making her smile. Always a good sign, right?

"So" she started "Last time I was asking about your divorce, before you disappeared on me" She took another sip of her drink and looked at me expectantly.

"Yes, sorry. You'd gone by the time I'd finished" I replied. "What did you want to know?"

"Nothing really, I just know it can be an awful time. My sister got divorced a few years ago, and her ex committed suicide a few months later."

I didn't know what to say. I was a bit taken aback.

Can she see that you tried it? Surely not.

"Oh, I'm sorry" she blushed "I wasn't trying to be awful. I just know how bad it can get. She treated him badly, denied him access to my niece, and took his house. I can only imagine how he must have felt."

"It can get bad" I simply responded.

"Jesus, I feel terrible now. I'm such an idiot" she seemed genuinely upset.

"Don't worry" I said, smiling "I'm through the bad stage now. "I had someone watching over me" I nodded back towards Steve.

"You're lucky to have such a good friend" she said, the relief obvious to see.

"Yes. Yes, I am."

"She looked at the clock on the wall and said in a mild panic "Sugar! I've got to get back. I'm supposed to be making dinner" She stood and put her coat on.

She turned to me and smiled. "I had a good time, thank you"

"Me too" I said with a grin.

"I'm sorry I have to go, hopefully see you again soon?"

"I really hope so"

Big smile. "Text me? You know, just to let me know you're ok"

I laughed. "I'll do that"

She smiled, waved, and left the café.

"She seems nice" Steve walked over, drying a cup.

"Yeah, she is" I said "Oddly enough, that's exactly what she said about you too"

"Good taste that one, she's a fucking keeper mate"
"I told her she was out of her mind"
"Fuck you. Now get out, I want to go home."
"You have a home?" I asked jokingly "Rumour has it you live here"
"Yeah, rumour also has it you're a dick. Get out".
We laughed, hugged, and I went off home.
I'd had a good day and thought Chrissy had too. Happy days, I didn't fuck it up.

I got home, and picked up the post; bill, advert, and other garbage. Nothing official, all good. Nothing was going to spoil my mood today. I text the kids to see how they were and made myself some dinner. Quick and easy stir fry. Fired up the laptop whilst eating to check on work. Couple of new jobs from clients, and the usual spam. As long as the jobs kept coming in, I was happy. There was an email from the prospective client I mentioned earlier, asking if we could do a Teams meeting to go through some details. I had a look at my calendar and replied with a few times/dates that worked best for me. Wouldn't get a response till Monday, which gave me a few days to get my sales pitch sorted, and wonder about what it was they wanted to go through.

After dinner, I grabbed a beer, and went through some online editing classes. It always paid to keep up to date and relevant. They cost a fair bit, but the qualifications were always worth having in case clients wanted a cv. Tiredness overtook me eventually, and I decided enough was enough. I shut down and went to bed. No problems falling asleep tonight.

Mr Holmes could wait till tomorrow.

DAY 9

Sunday, 9th of March.

Sunday morning, 08.15. I opened the curtains and stuck my head out the window. It was still snowing, which I didn't have a problem with. The village was always dead-on Sundays, but the snow made it quieter still. Earie. Spooky. I got dressed and put some coffee in a thermos mug. I wanted to go for a walk down the tow path in the quiet. Call me mad, but it appealed to me. I got my coat and hat and stepped out into the cold. Wow. It really was cold. I grabbed a scarf too and started walking. The snow crunched loudly under my boots; the earie silence made it seem louder than usual. No tyre tracks on the road, just fresh snow. The path was empty, and there were no footprints or tracks to be seen. The silence was deafening. I was loving every second. Walking along, sipping my ever-chilling coffee, I had a sudden urge to build a snowman. Dunno why, but I just wanted to. I went onto the field at the side and started rolling the snowballs. This was fun! Felt like a child again. I finished Harry with a few twigs I snapped off the bare trees lining the field. Not a bad effort. I snapped a quick picture and sent it to Chrissy. Fucking hell, I was cold. Brrrr. Enough was enough. I retraced my footsteps back to the house and had a long, hot shower.

I decided to have breakfast at home, as Steve usually did his books on Sundays, so liked to be alone. I had a feeling that wasn't going to be a problem today, with the snow and all. I put some music on and made some toast. Got a reply from Chrissy, three smiley faces. Good enough I suppose. I finished and went up to the office to look at the jobs that came in yesterday. Nothing too bad. Another gear review, and a lesson about modes. Too technical for me. Never understood musical theory. Hopefully, would get a couple more jobs as the day progressed; they usually came in on Sundays.

I called my folks to make sure they were ok and see if they needed anything. Dad said they were ok, they had shopping delivered Friday, so wouldn't need anything. Besides, this was no weather to go out, he said. I told them to keep warm and let me know if they needed anything. I text the kids to make sure they were ok, both good. One complaining about cancelled football lesson, the other happy but wishing she could go see her friends. Apparently, they weren't to go out today, as the weather was too bad.

Steve called to ask if I knew much about employment laws and paying NI contributions, as he was completely lost. Sorry mate, not my forte. He used some very choice words to "thank" me for getting him to take on help, wished me well, and went off in search of help online.

Out of sheer boredom, I decided to make a start on the instructional video. It was my day off, but, what else was there to do? I could waste away my day sitting behind the tv, or gaming, but decided work was more important.

A few more jobs arrived as I was editing, and a message about a possible new client. One of my existing guys, knew a guy that did piano instruction online, and was looking to make his content more professional. I opened the attachment and made a few notes whilst the guy was telling students how to use 7th chords for dramatic effect. Again, musical theory wasn't my thing, and neither was piano. I emailed the client back saying I would have a go at the video and send it back tomorrow, as a free sampler. Hopefully he would be impressed, and I would be able to add another client name to my books.

At 14.00, I decided to call it a day. I could finish the sampler in the morning. It needed a little more work, and it would be done. I went down to the kitchen and made myself a cup of tea.

Checked my phone; nothing. Had a bit of cleaning to do after my tea was gone, and I was keen to get on and get it over with. That only took about an hour. Bored again. Checked my phone; still nothing. *Wait, what are you expecting exactly? She responded already. Chill man.*

As soon as I put my phone down, it buzzed. It was James, wanting to know if I was watching the football. I told him I'd forgotten but would go watch now. I grabbed some water and went to the lounge to watch the football; 15 minutes till kick-off. I had completely forgotten about the football match. To be honest, I wasn't massively into football, but would watch a Liverpool game if I had time. Today, I had time. I text Steve to see if he fancied watching the match, and he said he was already in the pub. Ah, I meant here. That meant going out into the cold. *And being around lots of people heheheheh!* Shut up inner voice! What the hell; it would be fun. I turned off the tv, got my hat, coat, and scarf (LFC), and made my way to the pub as fast as the conditions would allow.

The pub was warm, and surprisingly crowded for a Sunday. In a blizzard. Steve spotted me and called me over; he had secured a prime table in front of the screen. Jason waved, signalling he would bring a pint over. I spotted my neighbour Mark, who raised his glass to me, and a few more familiar faces; all very warm, and welcoming. I loved small village life. Sat down next to Steve who gave me a big hug "Good to see you bud" he said, apparently a few pints ahead of me... The match was great; we were 3-1 up at half-time. Time for the loo. I made my way through the crowd to the gents, where I had to join a small queue of like-minded guys. On my way back, someone called out my name, I turned to see who it was; old Bill from my previous job. I waved at him, shouted that I'd see him after the match. I turned back to carry on and found myself face-to face with Chrissy.

"Jesus!" I shouted in shock.

"That bad?" she laughed.

"Sorry, I didn't see you there".

"No worries. You with someone?" A leading question? *Is she checking on you?*

"Just Steve, we're watching the match" I nodded towards the screen on the back wall.

"Ah, well, you enjoy the match Jack, and I'll see you on Friday" *Shit. She's leaving?*

"Wait. You're leaving?"

"Yes, my aunt's friend has offered to take me to Ramsey in his tractor, I can get the bus from there."

"A tractor?"

"Yes, great, isn't it? Don't think I've ever been in one before" She smiled enthusiastically.

She looked fantastic. Wow. Wait, you've had a few beers, Jack; think before engaging mouth!

"I was hoping you'd have to stay" I said, a bit disappointed.

"Work to do Jack, can't do it from here yet. You take care, and don't forget to text me. Ok?"

"Yeah, of course". She gave me a quick hug, and walked over to the door, where her aunt was waiting. They both waved and then they were gone. Shit. Fuck. Balls. Depressed, I made my way back to Steve, and lost myself in the match.

We won the game comfortably, and I said my goodbyes, then went over and had a quick chat with old Bill, before making my way back home. The snow was falling heavily, but I could make out the tractor tyre marks on the road. She was gone. I walked home in a bit of a funk and had to have a hot shower to warm up. I sobered up a bit and filled up my water bottle. I plonked down on the sofa with a cup of tea and some toast. Pulled my phone from my pocket and saw that I had 2 texts from Chrissy. First one just to let me know she had gotten home ok, and the second to tell me not to worry; she'd be back Friday. With a smiley face. That cheered me up a bit, and I watched a bit of crappy tv till bedtime.

I lay in bed, my mind a whirl. I put my headphones in and started listening, but lost track pretty quickly. There was a very brief hug. *But deffo a hug, right?* It was quick, but I remember the smell of her perfume. Not sure wha... Wait a minute! I pulled my headphones out. She said she "couldn't work from here yet". YET. Did that mean she was moving here? Or bringing her work gear with her so she could stay longer? I didn't really care which it was; she would be here.

That was enough.

Happiness.

I stuck my headphones back in and fell asleep in Victorian London.

DAY 10

Monday, 10th of March.

I woke up in a depressed state this morning; I missed my kids. A sadness that brought me close to tears had enveloped me. Today was not going to be a good day. Sigh. I got up and couldn't even be bothered to get on the treadmill. After I had showered and dressed, I found myself in the kitchen, wrapped in a blanket, clutching a cold coffee, staring out of the window. The house was completely silent. I was sinking.
Shit.
I should do something. I should. Can't be bothered though. I needed my kids. I needed to see them. Wasn't going to happen.

Minor tangent. This is one of those examples I mentioned where you have mini relapses after acceptance. You get this sudden black cloud of complete and utter sadness that closes around

you. No matter what you do, you can't shake it off. You feel like a total failure. You've let your kids down. You're less than useless. The outside world ceases to exist, and you get trapped in a web of depression.
THIS is why you need a constant support network, or even just one person that checks up on you every day. You may get sick of them asking, but it's important. Trust me on that one. I was lucky, I had……

Loud banging on the front door roused me from my depressive funk. What? Who? I trudged to the door and opened it, still wrapped in a blanket. "Fucking hell mate, answer your fucking phone would you! You ok?" He looked me up and down. "Of fuck. No, you're not ok. Come here" He came in and gave me a massive bear hug. I didn't care who it was, could have been anybody; I just let go and sobbed like a child.
"It's gonna be ok mate. It's gonna be ok".
He was right; it *was* going to be ok. But right now, at this precise moment; it *wasn't*. And I was glad to have him here.

After a couple of minutes, I slowly broke away. He pulled out a chair and told me to sit in it. I did what I was told whilst he busied himself in the kitchen. "It's like a fucking morgue in here man, that doesn't help" He put the heating on, opened the blinds, and proceeded to replace my cold coffee with a hot espresso.

"Get that down you" I obeyed. It felt good. "After that, you're coming with me. Have a decent breakfast where I can keep my eye on you"
"What time is it?" I managed.
"It's five past ten mate. I've been calling you since half eight. Where's your phone?"
"Upstairs. I think". He went off to retrieve my phone.
A few moments later, he was back. "Here" he handed me the phone "You have some messages too, check them" He took the blanket from me, and was busy putting my shoes on me as I went through the messages. My mum, James, Chrissy. Countless missed calls from Steve. Shit, what the fuck is wrong with me?
I put my coat and hat on, and we walked over to Steve's cafe. I felt safe. I felt loved.
It wasn't overly busy when we got there, the morning rush was over. Willow was smiling from behind the counter. "Morning" she said as we walked in. It was warm and familiar inside. It felt like home.
"Have a seat, and I'll sort you out" He led me to my usual place, and sat me down. I felt at peace. The cloud was slowly lifting. Got my phone out and answered my mum and James; mum was checking in, and James was asking for some money for football boots. Chrissy. Wanting to know if I was ok. I text everyone back and transferred some money to my son's account.
"Here you go" a cheerful voice said, putting a

cappuccino in front of me.
"Thank you, Willow," She walked off, and I took a sip. "Willow?"
"Yes?" I stood up and walked over to the counter. I stuck out my hand, and she took it.
"Jack. Pleased to meet you."
"Nice to meet you too Jack" she smiled.
"That, " I said nodding behind me "Is the best cappuccino I've ever had"
A broad grin "Thank you"
"No, thank *you*" I said. "He's lucky to have you".
"Who's lucky to have who?" Steve asked, emerging from the little kitchen.
"*You* are lucky to have Willow" I told him. "That cappuccino over there? It's the best I've had"
"Fuck me, better than mine?"
"Mate, anyone's is better than yours" He flicked me the finger.
"Perked up eh mate? Good to see man, good to see" he turned to Willow "And *you*. You have to show *me* how to make *that*" pointing towards my drink.
"Not sure I can teach an old dog new tricks" she replied coyly.
Steve stood gobsmacked. "Fuck's sake"
"You'll fit in nicely" I winked at her.
He turned to me "Take this and sit the fuck down" he handed me a plate with 2 sausage baps on it.
"You're my hero mate" I said and walked off.
"Old fucking dog...?" I heard him mutter behind me.

I finished my breakfast and told Steve it was time for me to get home to work. "You going to be ok?" he asked. "I am now mate. Thank you" I hugged him and walked home a new man.

Back at home. In my office. Lost in work. I finished off the sampler video and sent it back to the client. Fingers crossed. Checked my inbox to see what was left for the week. Appointment for tomorrow from the prospective client. Instant nerves. Few more jobs to finish before Friday. Going to be a busy boy this week, but the money was always welcome. I opened up the instructional video and continued my editing.

Lunchtime came and went. I finished the job at around 15.00. I needed to get out for air. Went downstairs and put my hat and coat on. Checked my phone, James thanking me for the cash, heart emoji from my mum. I had a sudden urge to ask Chrissy what her name was, as I still wasn't sure. Christine? Made sense. Decided to ask anyway. Sent the message, put phone in pocket, and went for a walk. It was freezing, but the crisp, cold air was exactly what I needed. It had stopped snowing; the landscape was beautiful. I took a few pictures on my phone. The council had cleared the road to Ramsey, but it was eerily quiet. Can't blame anyone I thought. It's no weather for driving. Got back home fully recharged.

Lost the coat and shoes, and crashed on the sofa.

Checked my phone.
There was a message from Chrissy; her name was Christelle.
Wow.
What a beautiful name.
I told her as much.
This led to a lengthy text conversation:

Her: (blush emoji) Thank you. It's French.
Me: French?
Her: Yes, my mother is French.
Her: Lenoir, before you ask
Me: ?
Her: surname. I took Mum's name after dad left.
Me: I'm sorry
Her: don't be. Happy to talk about it Friday. You can buy me a coffee ;-)
Her: how are you doing today?
Me: now? Great. This morning, terrible.
Her: oh no! What happened?
Me: got depressed about not seeing the kids.
Her: that must be really hard for you
Me: yes, it is. I can put it out of my mind a lot of the time, but it catches up.
Her: I'm sorry
Me: it's ok. Steve came and rescued me
Her: he's a good friend
Me: yes, he is. The best
Her: (picture) view from the window ☹

Picture of busy, wet road. Lots of people about. Typical city scene.

I sent back a picture I took on my walk of a pristine snowy landscape.

Me: ugh!
Her: I know ☹
Me: (picture) went for some air, beautiful out.
Her: wow! I miss it already. Be there soon though
Me: You fancy roast dinner at the pub on Sunday? If you're still here.
Her: I'll be there. Yes, sounds great ☺
Her: work call. Got to go! Take care x.
Me: you too

And she was gone. Wow. That was a quick chat in reality, but lots of information to process.

- Christelle Lenoir. What an absolutely beautiful name.
- Her dad had left them
- She wants to talk about it
- She misses being here
- She cares
- She'll be here Sunday afternoon

I dwelled on the last one for a bit. Does that mean she's going later Sunday or Monday morning? Does it mean she's able to stay longer? She can work from here? Full of happiness, I went back upstairs and immersed myself in work. Bliss.

No post worth mentioning today, by the way. Postman was good to me.

I decided to call it quits at 4. It would be good to

go see how my parents were coping. I text mum to see if I could come for dinner. Of course. Told her I would leave shortly, is there anything she needed on my way over? No thank you, just yourself.
I had a fantastic butter chicken and catch-up with my folks. Caught up on all the gossip and avoiding questions about my wellbeing. Mum knew not to push too hard, and I wasn't about to tell her about Chrissy. Not yet. There wasn't much to tell anyway. She was a friend. I guess I could consider her a friend now, right? I thought so. A friend. A beautiful friend.

Got back from parents around 7. Put the box of leftovers in the fridge and grabbed myself a beer.
Quick check of emails. Yes! The sampler had gone down well, and the client wanted to go ahead. Could I send him the paperwork? I responded with the relevant contract attachments. Happy days. Not a massive income stream, but it all counts.

Phone buzzing......Gloria.
"Hi Gloria"
"Hi Jack"
"What's up?"
"Helen wants to know if you're able to have the kids this Friday instead of Wednesday as she wants to take them to the theatre. She managed to get tickets for that play Elsie wants to see."

Shit. Friday? I wasn't going to say no, but it would make things awkward. I wasn't ready for them to see me with another woman. (Even though we were only friends.)

"You still there?"
"Yeah, of course, not a problem."
"You sure?"
"I have a work thing Friday but will shift it to Wednesday. It's all good. Tell her it's ok"
"Ok Jack"
"Thanks Gloria"
"Jack...?"
"Yes?"
"Everything ok?"
"All good. Thanks Gloria"
"Ok. Bye Jack"
"Bye"

Shit. I'd have to have a chat with Chrissy to see if we could meet up another day. *How you going to explain that you don't want to be seen with them?* Not strictly true, but I wasn't ready for my kids to see that yet. *Is that normal?* I didn't know and had nobody to ask. I decided to stick with it.

I'm sure she wouldn't have a problem with it. *Would she?* Nah, why would she? Dunno.

Mini tangent time...
Throughout the divorce, I found keeping everybody happy really, really difficult. It's like traversing a minefield, blindfolded. You have to be soooo careful with what you say, as you don't want to piss anyone off. Not just keeping everyone

happy but making sure you tell the right people the right information. Even after the divorce, nowadays, I find it hard. If you miss anyone out on any kind of communication, the trouble it causes! Wow. A juggling act. And I can't juggle. At all.

And we're back in the room....

I went over what I would say to Chrissy whilst "watching" some tv. After an hour or so, I had it worked out in my head. I had also been wondering why Gloria was asking if everything was ok. Fuck. Hopefully, this wouldn't keep me awake most of the night.

Shit.

It did.

Even Sherlock Holmes couldn't rescue me.

DAY 11

Tuesday, 11th of March.

Oh Man. What a shit night. Woke up, if you can call it that, and got straight into my running kit. I knew I needed to do my run, or my day would go to shit. I filled my water bottle and did a 6k run.

I was going to stop at 5, but felt like I needed to push a bit harder. After a long shower, I got dressed and went up to the office.

After an hour or so of working on the gear review video, I heard the letterbox rattle. Good time for a break. I went down, picked up the post, and went to the kitchen. Bill, crap, solicitor, charity. Solicitor. Shit. Never good. Got a moment for a quick one about solicitors?

Yeah, why not.

So, who can afford a solicitor? Not me. Well, I

could, but I wasn't going to waste my money, as I knew that as a man, legally, I was lower than dog shit. Before she left, we agreed most things; custody, child support etc. After I kicked her out, she went to live with that prick. He obviously whispered in her ear, and before you know it, I started receiving solicitor's letters. How the hell can she afford that? She doesn't work. Legal aid. Genius. Thank you benefit system. Whereas I would have to pay £800 just for a formal response through a solicitor (per letter mind!), EVERYTHING was free for her. I was basically being financially blackmailed into agreeing with her terms & demands. You don't have to; we can always settle it in court....... £££££££££. Going to court would bankrupt me, but she gets it all for free. I love how the system is so fairly balanced. Basically, I didn't want to throw money away, so represented myself legally. I'd rather keep my money for my kids. She didn't have to worry about that.

Custody:
 -Before solicitor: shared, whenever the kids wanted.
 -After solicitor: sole custody, weekends only.

Child support:
- Before solicitor: £200 per child, per month. (just over what the CSA recommended)
- After solicitor: £250 per child, plus £200 for her, per month, and 50% of my pension upon

retirement.

I received a letter from her solicitor with all this officially in writing, for me to agree and sign.

This was all before she blocked me, so I was able to speak to her direct and tell her that it wasn't what we had agreed to, and it was totally unreasonable. She was already getting more than the CSA would give her, and my pension was mine. Why would she be entitled to it? I told her she could have all the child benefit for both kids, as I thought she would need it more than me. To my complete surprise, she actually agreed. She said her solicitor had pressured her into it, and it wasn't her idea. I wasn't sure if I believed that or not, but still asked her to reconsider. She agreed to get her solicitor to drop it and revert to the original agreement. And she did. Fucking solicitors.

Rant over. Just typing it out made me angry again!

Back to the story…

I opened the solicitor's letter; Dear Mr. Beckett…. blah, blah, blah… It was just to let me know that the decree absolute was still on track for issue on the 17th. Thanks. Wonder how much they charged the Government to send that out? GRRRRRRR. (Oh, yeah, Jack Beckett. At your service. Not mentioned my surname before)

6 days and I was free of this shit. 6 days. You got this Jack.

I made myself a cheese toastie and a cup of tea, then went back to work. Nothing was going to ruin my day today. Especially a fucking solicitor. I managed to finish another video by 4 o'clock, which was long enough today. 2 days to do 3 videos. Doable. Might even do a bit more later. But, for now, I needed to get out. I shut down, grabbed my coat, and went out. Needed a few bits and pieces from the shop and would call in to see Steve whilst I was out. Got most of what I wanted at the shop, but they only had full fat milk, would have to do. Steve was ok, full of praise for young Willow, and full of colourful language. As always. All was good. But, did I have a minute?

"Sure mate, what's up?"

"I seriously need fucking help with this employment shite. I don't know what the fuck I'm doing"

"What kind of things you worried about?"

"The national insurance, holiday, sick pay, all that bollocks" He was getting animated, and obviously worried.

"Ok mate, relax. I know it's important, let's try sort it out."

I pulled out my phone and called old Bill, who had helped me to set up my own business.

"Hi Jack, how are you coping?" Seriously, did everyone know what was going on in my life??

"I'm good thanks mate. How are you?"

"Surviving, you know. Place isn't the same after

you left" he bemoaned.
"I bet it isn't" (laughs) "Got a favour to ask"
"Shoot"
"You know Steve right?"
"Cafe Steve, sure."
"Yeah, he's just taken on a girl to help out, and he needs some help with all the Employer/Employee stuff. You able to help?"
"Give me his number, I'll call him right away."
"Cheers Bill." I relayed the number to Bill, thanked him, and hung up.
"There mate, sorted. He's going to call you right away" As I spoke the words, his phone rang
"Hi Bill. Yeah, would be grateful if you could" he sat down at a table, and got lost in conversation & furious not scribbling. I gave him a thumbs up & left. Felt good to be able to give something back, however small.

Where to go now? Probably home would be an idea as I was still carrying a bag of shopping. Slow walk home. Snow started falling earlier, but not too heavy. There was about a foot and a half in places. Hadn't seen this much snow in years. Where's this global warming everyone keeps going on about? I turned into the main street and spotted Mary walking slowly towards the shop. I picked up speed, and got to her just before she went inside.
"Oh, hi Jack"
"Hi Mary. You ok?"
"This cold isn't helping my hip, but I'm okay

otherwise." she laughed

"Yeah, I know what you mean"

"Behave. You're too young for old people aches and pains" she said mockingly

"Guess you're right. Hey, here, let me give you my number. If you ever need anything when Chrissy isn't here, please let me know. I'm happy to help, it's no bother." I handed her a business card from my wallet.

"You're very kind Jack thank you. I may take you up on your offer if this weather continues"

"It's no bother, so please don't hesitate. Anyway, I'll let you get inside and get warm, nice to see you".

"And you, take care" she said with a wave.

She disappeared inside, and my happiness moved up a level. I didn't really know Mary, but I was always willing to help anyone. Regardless.

My brain: *Jack, get home. It's fucking freezing.*

Me: You're right.

After I got home and put the shopping away, I went back up to the office. I may as well do a bit more work I thought. The more I do today, the less I'll have to do tomorrow. Besides, I was in a good mood. Helping Steve out of a jam really made me happy. He'd done so much for me lately. I owed him.

I made a start on another gear review video, and was pleasantly surprised to find it was on a guitar I actually owned. I watched it all the way through, and had an idea. I had a DSLR, so thought I'd try a inserting a few close-ups over some of the narration. I was able to get some great shots, and inserting them made the video 200% better in my opinion. Hopefully the client shared this view.... I finished it, and emailed it out. Fingers crossed.

Pretty chuffed with my efforts, I shut down, and went to watch some more 24. I was in the mood for a bit of Jack Bauer. I got myself a bottle of ale, and a pack of crisps.

After about ten mins of 24, my phone buzzed. Chrissy.

Her: Hey you, how you doing?
Me: I've actually had a great day, so pretty happy. How about you?
Her: Wow, that's great, mine has been proper boring. Work, work, work.
Me: Know the feeling, I've just finished. Sat down with a beer watching some 24
Her: Oh I love Jack Bauer. Which season you watching?
Me: Season 1, started from scratch
Her: Cool. I hear you bumped into Aunt Mary earlier
Me: News travels fast!
Her: Lol. She said you were lovely
Me: She has good taste obviously
She: She needs new glasses me thinks
Me: Eh? Thanks.
Her: ☐
Me: I need to ask something
Her: uh-oh.... :-s

Me: Nothing terrible, don't worry.
Her: What is it?
Me: My soon to be ex has asked if I could have the kids Friday instead of Wed
Her: Ah, hey, it's cool. I'll be here Saturday
Me: You sure?
Her: Of course, you have a great day with your kids.
Me: Thanks. Was a bit worried
Her: Why?
Me: Didn't know how you'd react
Her: Spending time with your kids is important, especially at the moment. I can wait.
Me: You're lovely, thanks
Her: You have good taste obviously
Me: Or I need glasses....
Her: Hey!
Me: Lol
Her: I'm off to bed, early meeting tomorrow
Me: Enjoy! Night
Her: night Jack Beckett x

I put down my phone with a massive grin on my face.

If my day wasn't good enough already, it was interstellar now.
Christelle Lenoir. More than a beautiful name.

I finished my beer and went to bed.
Needless to say..... I slept like a log.

Zzzzzz......

DAY 12

Wednesday, 12th of March.

I was up and about early, as the kids were coming today. The kids are coming today! I know I went into this during last Friday's chapter, but it's difficult to put into words how happy it made (makes) me.

The house was immaculate. As always. I'd been for a run, showered, had breakfast, and was ready. It was only 10 o'clock, and they weren't getting here for another hour. I had time to go up to the office and do a quick bit of work.

Then…

Wait…

Shit… They're not coming till Friday.

I crashed immediately.
Fucking hell. No, no, no, no, no! Not today, please.

Not today. Not today.
Sinking.
Please. Stop.
Still sinking.
I sat on the stairs, and cried for almost an hour.

After I ran out of tears, I decided I wasn't going to let my day turn to shit. I was going to be *better* than that. I was going to be *stronger* than that. *Pick yourself up Jack*. I did exactly that. I went to the kitchen, picked up my phone, and called the only person that could save me.

"What's up mate?"
"Tell me it's going to be ok."
"Shit. Mate. It's going to be ok. You're going to get through this. You're stronger than you think."
"Thanks"
"You'll be ok"
"I know"
I hung up. He was right of course, I *was* going to be ok. But at that moment in time, I had my doubts.
I grabbed my laptops, grabbed my coat, and went to my safe place.

I sat in the café window for the rest of the afternoon. Steve kept me fuelled with food & drink. And most importantly; support. Just being there, knowing he was ready to catch me, made all the difference in the world. I finished all but 1 of my jobs, which meant I had a lot of time off tomorrow. I needed to fill my time, to avoid another stall. I needed something. I emailed my prospective big fish client to see if they could make that meeting happen tomorrow afternoon. Almost instant response. Jack, no problem. 13.00 on Teams. That worked perfectly. I accepted. Gratefully.

Now I just needed to make sure I was ok today. I felt like I was still only at the halfway point, my emotions and head were all over the place.
Bold move time.

I text Chrissy.
Me: Hi, how are you today?

A few minutes later...

Her: Hey you! I'm fine, just finished work. How are you?
Me: Bad.
Her: Oh no! What happened??
Me: got myself ready for the kids this morning, then remembered they weren't coming till Fri
Me: I crashed

No reply. Instead, my phone rang.

"I needed to hear you say that you're ok"

My angel
I started to cry.

"Hey, hey, its ok, it's going to be ok" she said, her voice full of warmth

"I miss them so much" I blubbered
"I know you do. They know that too. A few more days, then things will be better"

She was right. Once finalised, the kids were free to come and go as they pleased. Helen had asked that the kids be involved as little as possible until it was all officially closed out. To her, and her solicitor, that meant I see them once a week only. *Bitch*. For once, you're right brain.

"I know. It just hurts so much"
"I'm sorry I'm not there for you"
"It's not your fault. Besides, Steve gives the best hugs ever"
"Well, I guess that means you don't need me there at all then" she said jokingly.
"I wish you *were* here" I said
"Couple of days. Have faith."

It was working. I was rising. This woman really was an angel.

"Thank you" I said.
"Any time. Really, call me any time you need to. I'll be here for you."
"See you Saturday"
"Yes you will. Count on it. Take care Jack Beckett"
"You too Christelle Lenoir"

I hung up. I felt rejuvenated. I felt normal. I felt loved. I felt alive again.
I packed my stuff, gave Steve a big hug, and

reassurance that I was in a good place, then went home.

Once I had put my gear away, I stood in the kitchen. Thinking. No! Danger! Danger! Do something! Quick! I went upstairs, got changed, put some loud music on, and jumped on the treadmill. Not sure my legs agreed with this course of action, but fuck them. I needed something.
I managed 4k, and was done. Physically and mentally. I showered, and went down to make myself some dinner. Just as I opened the fridge, the doorbell rang. I was expecting a few deliveries, so hoped this would be one of those. I was wrong, in a way.
I opened the door.

"Chinese?" Steve. The man who knew exactly how to keep me flying high. This time holding up two bags full of Chinese takeaway. (There's a takeaway in Ramsey, before you ask…)
"You fucking star" I said, letting him in.
We ate, had a few beers, and talked about good times.

Steve left at about 10, and I went to my bed a happy, contented man.
I lay in bed with my headphones in, thinking about how lucky I was. Yes, I was in a shit place, but I had that support network I talked about. Remember that? It's so important. Even if you only have one person you can turn to. Use that outlet. If

you have nobody; phone someone like Samaritans. Don't be scared of opening up. Don't be scared of showing emotion. Can't stress that enough. You're a man, not a fucking statue. Nobody will think you're weak; the opposite is true. They will think you are strong. That you have the strength to push through the "macho barrier", and show how you feel. It's liberating.

Moriarty had just been to see Sherlock at 221b, famously saying "I can promise you the one. But not the other" before he stormed out in a huff.

The Final Problem. This divorce was a bit like a final problem for me.
And, like Moriarty, I can say this:

I can promise you it will get better, but not without relapses.

Spoiler alert for your future: you'll cope with relapses. You will. Trust me.

Goodnight.

DAY 13

Thursday, 13th of March.

Today is going to be interesting. Just saying.

I woke and silenced my chiming alarm. Good day today Jack, I said to myself. I got up, opened the curtains. Blue sky. Sun. I opened the window; freezing. The cold air felt good.

Decided against a run as I did one last night. Instead, I went for a walk over to Steve's to get a coffee and some pastries to takeaway. Steve was out, so just Willow in the café. We chatted whilst she made my cappuccino. She was loving working with Steve, it was all so different to the place in the city. I bade her farewell, and walked back to the house.

I set the bag of breakfast on the table, and hung up my coat. The coffee was still hot-ish, thankfully. I gave it a 10 sec blast in the microwave regardless. I sat back, and enjoyed it. It was good. Instant mood lift.

I finished up, and went up to finish my work for the week. I flashed up the pc, and loaded up my project. The letterbox rattled. Bit early for the posty I thought. Went down to see what it was. When I say it, my heart sank. A letter. *Helen's handwriting*. I picked it up, and opened the door. Had a look around, but nobody to be seen. I could see her footprints in the snow.

Closed the door and sat at the kitchen table staring at the envelope. Feels like deja bloody vue, I thought. *What the fuck is this now*? Only one way to find out.

I opened it, and took out the folded note. There were obvious smudges to the ink in a few places, like she'd been crying or something. She had. Read for yourself:

Jack,

I know I'm the last person you're expecting to hear from right now, but I felt like I needed to share this with you, as you have a right to know. I've just discovered that Ian was seeing someone behind my back, the whole time I've known him. You should know that I left him immediately, and that we're now living at my parents place until I find us somewhere to live. Again.

I feel like a total failure. I feel like I've ruined

the lives of everyone around me. Don't worry, I'm not going to beg you to take me back, I know we're beyond that now. I will get back on my feet, and try to make life as good as I can for the children.

I'm sorry Jack. I'm so, so sorry. You deserved none of this. And it's all been for nothing.
Helen.

(See? Interesting. Told you.)

What the Fuck!

What the Fuck!

What the Fuck!

What the Fuck!

What the hell was I supposed to think?? What the fuck did I just read???
Fucking bitch! She's ruined your life. For nothing!
I was sooooooooooooo fucking angry. I shouted, threw my breakfast across the room, then got my coat and ran out the door.
Tinkle...
"Back agai....." I cut him off before he could finish
"Kitchen, now"
I stormed past him, straight into the little kitchen in the back
"The fuck's wrong with you?" he said, confused
"Read this" I thrust the letter in his hand.

"What is it?" he asked, then looked at it. "Oh. Shit. Helen?"
"Yes, fucking Helen. Have a read"
"Alright mate, calm down". He read the letter. "Fuck me..."
"I know right. What the fuck is that bitch thinking? I'm fucking livid"
"Yeah, I can see that" he read the letter again.
"But, erm mate" he said
"What?"
"*This* is fucking brilliant!" he beamed, indicating the letter.
"What? How is it fucking brilliant?" My anger was now mixed with a tinge of confusion.
"Can't you see what she's done here?" Steve asked, waving the letter in his hand.
"I don't want her back Steve" I said angrily
"No mate, not that. She's handed you an *ace* here buddy" he said with a grin.
I was confused. An ace? What the hell did he mean? I had expected him to explode into my levels of anger, not be all happy about it.
"Eh? What are you talking about?" I asked
"Simple mate. See this here?" held up the letter
"This is your permanent get-out-of-jail card"
"I'm not following" Still confused. *Man has a point.* Shut up inner voice!
"Mate, whenever she tries to do anything to screw you over, or has a go at you for something, you pull out this baby right here" again, waving of the letter.

"Like blackmail?"

"No mate, like a permanent moral high-ground pass" He handed the letter back "Keep that fucking safe somewhere"

"Dude, think of it this way; it's a win-win for you. She broke up your marriage to be with that prick and turns out he was cheating on her the whole time she was cheating on you. It's instant fucking karma" Expectant look... "Brilliant...?"

"Yeah, you know what mate, you're right" I said, nodding slowly.

He was right. Why didn't I see it that way? Why was I angry? I was so blinded by rage, that I didn't see the letter for what it really was. Steve looked relieved, like I'd seen the light at last.

"Stupid fucker, serves her right" Steve said.

"You're not wrong buddy." I put the letter in my pocket and apologised. "Sorry mate, I was just so bloody angry"

He put his hands on my shoulders "Never apologise. We are mates, brothers. We're here for each other."

"Thanks" I said sheepishly.

"Now sit the fuck down and I'll get Willow to get us coffee" He ushered me out, and I went and sat in my usual place by the window. Steve was right, I did now have the moral high ground. She was on the defensive now. I know it shouldn't, but it made me feel great. Call it Schadenfreude if you want, but I don't care. She deserved this.

Steve came and sat with me. He had a couple of

pastries on a plate, and one sticking out of his mouth. "Here, eat these" he said, pushing the plate over to me. I was in no mood to refuse after throwing my breakfast at the window...
"You're not making the coffee?" I asked
He leaned in "Mate, I'm not being funny, but she's a fucking coffee wizard" he said
"Oh really?"
"She's fucking brilliant. Best thing you've ever made me do"
Willow came over and gave us each a Latte. "Heard that." big grin. "You ok Jack?" she asked.
"Yeah, I am now" I said, patting Steve on the shoulder.
"He's a peach this one" she said, and ruffled Steve's hair before retreating to the counter.
"The fuck just happened?" I asked Steve wide-eyed.
"Not a fucking clue mate" he said, clearly confused himself.
"She's really made herself at home" I said with a laugh "She'll be bossing *you* around before you know it!" I said, loud enough for Willow to hear.
"There's a clear divide here Jack" she said "This is my bit" Indicating the coffee machine and counter area "And that's his" nodding back towards the kitchen.
"Hey! I have feelings you know!" Steve said mockingly
"I'm sure you do, somewhere" Willow retorted.
Steve made a show of looking hurt.
"Looks like you have your work cut out there

buddy" I told him.

"Yeah, she's getting proper feisty"

Wait a minute. I knew that look. "She'd be perfect for you" I said.

"What? The fuck you talking about?" he said, pretending to look confused.

"You know what I mean"

"Mate, she's too young" he said

"Get out of it. She's only like 6 years younger than you, dumbass"

"5 actually" he said looking over at her.

"She likes you. It's obvious. Why don't you ask her out sometime?"

"You think?" he asked

"Yeah, life's too short mate. Time to hang up the Casanova boots and find yourself a girlfriend"

"You're probably right" he said with a sigh.

"I know I'm right" I got up, ruffled his hair, and left him to it.

"Later Willow!"

"Bye Jack" she called "See you tomorrow?"

"Probably"

When I got home, first thing I did was clear up the mess I'd made earlier on. Felt embarrassed I let myself go. Not like me at all. I guess a divorce changes a person forever. For better or worse.

Ooh, that's a good excuse for another tangent....

Does divorce change you as a person? I think it does. I was a carefree, outgoing, fun guy before the divorce. Now I think I'm just fundamentally sad.

People can see it in you, you're not the fun guy to be around that you once were. It's like an essential part of your personality has been cut out. *Much like your heart was cut out, then set on fire in front of you...* Yeah, thanks. It's quite sad really. Don't get me wrong, I'm not sad all the time, but find it incredibly easy to drift into a blue mood. Never used to have that. I was out all the time, meeting people, doing stuff. Now, I like to be home. I have to make an effort to stay in contact with friends and family now, whereas before it just came naturally. And what about love? Did it make me a cynic about love? Yes. I was in a kind of "I'll be single for the rest of my life" mind-set for a long time. I wasn't interested, didn't want to get hurt again, happy to be alone. My one little protective family group; just me and my kids. Then, completely out of the blue, someone comes into your life and turns your life upside-down.
It's amazing how love works.
It's amazing how life works.
Embrace it, don't fight it.

Anyways, after tidying up, I went up and checked my emails. Couple of questions and correction requests from clients. Reminder: Meeting in 15 mins. Shit! I'd completely forgotten. I ran down to the bathroom, brushed my teeth, and made sure I looked presentable.
I set up my camera and made sure the angles and audio were right. The chiming from my speakers

indicated it was time; time to sell yourself Jack. You got this.
I crossed my fingers and answered the call. "Afternoon Jack, nice to see you...."

Time to shine.

An hour later, I clicked on the disconnect button. Pfffffffffffff. I sat back with my hands behind my head. That was some call. It did, however, go extremely well. This was a well-known music retailer, and they seemed to like my office setup in the background, and the guitars hanging on the wall. "You're a musician Jack?" they had seemed impressed. Get in! They said they would email me within 24hrs to let me know their decision, as they had a couple of other people to consider.

I didn't really *need* this contract; I just *wanted* it. So bad. It would do wonders for my reputation and might lead to more work. *Oh. Wait. Could you handle more work*? Fuck it, I'd worry about that later.

My phone chimed.

Text from Chrissy "How you doing today? Better?"

Me: Started badly, but am good now ☐
Her: Badly? How come? Kids not coming?
Me: No, not the kids. I'll tell you all about it on Sat.
Her: Ok. You sure you're ok?
Me: I was ok, now I'm more than ok.
Her: You say the nicest things ☐
Me: I try

Her: You do ok, trust me.
A noise from behind me; incoming email.

Me: Hey, I gotta go, work thing. See you sat
Her: Can't wait. See ya. X

Smile. Big smile.

I turned to my screen, and opened the email. "Jack, just to follow on from the interview earlier… blah blah… We take great pleasure in informing you that the decision was unanimous; you're our guy. Please respond to this email if you would like to go ahead, and we'll get the legal people to send you the paperwork to sign. Etc. Etc."

Holy Fuck!

HOLY FUCK!

I jumped up and started shouting YES! YES! FUCKING YES!
I couldn't fucking believe it. I grabbed my phone and called Steve.
"S'up dude?"
"Pub tonight. We're celebrating" I said excitedly
"Whoa! What the fuck?" Steve asked.
"Mate, I've just landed a fucking HUGE contract" I beamed
"Fucking effort mate!"
"I'll tell you all about it later. It's fucking great" I was so excited.
"I can tell mate! See you there at 7?"
"See you there buddy" I hung up. I was on a

massive high. A MASSIVE high.
I called my folks and told them the good news. They were super happy for me; I'm sure my mum was crying when I hung up....

Still on a massive high, I changed into my running gear and smashed out a 6k run on the treadmill. It felt good. *I* felt good. For the first time in a while, my future was looking good. All bad thoughts were banished; this was MY time. Positivity time. Fuck you inner voice.
I showered, dressed, and made myself some dinner before heading out to meet Steve in the George.

Cut to: Interior of "The George" Pub.
Semi busy, a few locals scattered around. Jason, the bar man, stands behind the bar talking to one of the customers. In a corner, sat at a table, we find our two subjects; Jack and Steve. They appear to be in a celebratory mood, they are laughing, deep in conversation. Also, a small collection of empty pint glasses stand on the table, together with a few empty crisp packets. Camera moves in on this scene slowly....

"Mate, you have it together now. How will you cope with the extra work load though?
"Dunno yet, I'll manage somehow though."
"I'm sure you will. Do you have to declare this?"
"What?"
"You know, declare it to her..."
"The new job?"

"Nah, the extra income"

"No, we have an agreement already, it's all signed and official. No increases."

"Fucking hell, that's a good deal. How'd you manage that?"

"Her idea, not mine"

"Cheers to that"

Clinking glasses together....

"Happy for you man" Steve said

"Thanks dude, I'm really chuffed."

"So, in other news..."

"Yes?"

"I did what you suggested..."

"You took a barista course?"

"Dickhead. No. I asked Willow out"

"And???"

"She said she'd think about it"

"That sounds positive?"

"Yeah, I think so. Wasn't a no, right?"

"No, it wasn't. Just give her time. Don't push it." I offered

"I won't. Took all my courage just to ask. Not sure I could do it again." For a guy full of bravado, he sure was insecure when it came to relationships. But, he deserved happiness. He'd worked hard to get where he was, despite all the adversity he'd faced. He'd be a fine catch for any woman, and Willow seemed nice. She certainly liked him that was obvious. I had my fingers crossed for him.

"Time to call it a night mate, I have the kids

tomorrow, so don't want to be too hanging."
"Amen to that" He said and finished his pint.
We walked out and went our separate ways; Steve living a few doors down from my parents over the bridge, me in the opposite direction.

I got in, filled my water bottle, fed the cat, brushed my teeth, and went to bed.

No headphones required; I went out like a light.

DAY 14

Friday, 14th of March.

I was up and about early, as the kids were coming today. The kids are coming today! I know I went into this during Wednesday's chapter, but it's difficult to put into words how happy it made (makes) me.
The house was immaculate. As always. I'd been for a run, showered, had breakfast, and was ready. It was only 10 o'clock, and they weren't getting here for another hour. I had time to go up to the office and do a quick bit of work.

Just got to copy & paste that from Wed :-)

This time though there was no descent into the dark abyss; they really were coming today.
I had been feeling a little worse for wear, but a run and hot shower had sorted that out.
No plans for today, was just going to see what they

wanted to do. I did plan on taking them for lunch at Steve's, and just go from there.

We did just that. Both kids were more than happy to go see their uncle Steve, and we had a great time at the cafe. Steve was on top form, and he loved my kids like they were his own.

Tangent time…. Steve + Adversity. Let's go a bit deeper into that. Remember yesterday, at the pub, I mentioned that Steve deserved someone nice because of the adversity he'd faced? Well, let's have a look at that in more detail. Adversity. Shit. That's putting it lightly. He'd had his share. More than his share.

He'd been in a relationship with Jasmine for a few years. It was going great, although Jazz was a little insecure. They were perfect for each other. Him, the boisterous, happy guy, Her the quiet-ish, insecure girl. They brought the best out in each other. They decided they wanted to start a family, and it took a while, but Jazz finally got pregnant. Steve was over the moon; he was going to be a dad! They had rented a nice place together in Ramsey, and everything was perfect. But, and you knew there would be a "But", then it all started falling to pieces. It started when Jazz miscarried. They were both devastated, but Jazz took it particularly badly. She never recovered from it. She saw herself as a failure. Despite all the support and love Steve could give her, she spiralled out of control, and crashed. Hard. One day, Steve came home from

work, and called out for Jazz, but no response. Her mobile was on the kitchen table, with a note. He read the note, and his heart sank. He ran upstairs, but he was too late. She was gone. She looked peaceful, like she was sleeping; but she was gone. The note had explained how she couldn't live with the guilt of losing their child, and that he deserved someone better. He just about had the mind to call an ambulance before he lost it completely. I tried my best to get him back on his feet following the funeral, but it was a slow process. He was completely broken and had to be re-built from the ground up. I was there for him. *We* were there for him. Helen and I took him in, and saw to it that he received counselling, and all the love & support he needed. The day came eventually, when he wanted to stand on his own two feet. He used the money they had saved to buy their family home to buy the cafe, which at the time was empty, having previously been a fish & chip shop. It was just what he'd needed; a project he could completely dedicate himself to. He spent months gutting, rebuilding, and redesigning the inside to be a cafe.
The Cafe Jazz.
He deserves somebody good. The best in fact. And now you know why.
Back to the story…
We left Steve and Willow and headed for my parents' house. We spent an hour or so with them, which they loved. Mum missed seeing the kids, so any opportunity I could give her was greatly

appreciated. As we left, I asked the kids if they wanted to go for a walk along the canal, maybe build a snowman. Absolutely! We had so much fun; building snowmen, having snowball fights. It was a perfect afternoon. We went back to warm up and have dinner. I made us all spag-bol; the kid's favourite. We ate well and played Uno after. Then, all too soon, it was time for the last bus. I walked them to the bus stop, and waited with them till the bus came. I hugged them both fiercely, and they were gone.

I walked home feeling a bit down, but mostly full of happiness. It had been a great day, and I had loved every second of my time with them.

It was 21.38 when I got back, and I wasn't ready to call it a night just yet. I tidied, got myself a beer, and crashed in front of the telly. Nothing much on the box, so I put some music on instead. I picked up a guitar, and played along with some of the songs. I wasn't a great player, mostly rhythm, but I could hold my own. I'd been in a few bands in my younger years, but now only played casually. Very casually. Phone buzz…

Test from mum, asking if I had a good day with the kids. She just likes checking up on me I guess. We chatted for a bit, then she signed off to go to bed. I looked at my watch; 22.43. I thought about texting Chrissy, but thought it was likely too late to be doing that now. Tomorrow is another day.

I felt re-charged after seeing the terrible twosome, and I couldn't wait till next week; I'd get to see them more. Cue inner voice: *how much more do you think you'll be seeing them?* I didn't know to be honest. I would guess not so much during the week anymore as they'd be in school etc. Weekends sound like a cliché; Weekend Dad. But in reality, it worked perfectly for me. I would love to have them here for a few days a week. They could stay during the week, but the logistics didn't really work very well. They would have to be up super early in order to make it to school on time, and I didn't want to tire them out, just for my own benefit.

Lying in bed I got my headphones out, and was opening up the audio book app when a message came in from Chrissy. *This late?* Wow.

Her: Hi, how was your day?
Me: Hi, it was FANTASTIC thanks, we had a great day
Her: That's great ☐ you must be super happy
Me: I am, I feel like a different person.
Her: I saw you earlier, you were making snowmen on the tow path
Me: You did? I didn't see you
Her: I was walking Chico. We saw you from the bridge. Thought it best to stay away
Me: Sorry if it makes you feel bad
Her: Not at all ☐ I completely get it.
Me: That makes me happy

Her: Good. You still up for meeting tomorrow?
Me: Try stopping me
Her: Lol. When and where?
Me: Options are limited
Her: True! Cafe? After the morning rush, about 10?
Me: Absolutely.
Her: Ok, see you there. Goodnight, Jack Beckett x.
Me: Goodnight, Christelle Lenoir.

I put my phone and my headphones on the bedside table; wasn't going to need those tonight.

I fell asleep thinking happy thoughts of tomorrow.

DAY 15

Saturday, 15th of March.

I was awake early. Stupid early. The clock told me it was 06.09, and part of me wanted to just roll over and go back to sleep. The other part told me to get up; you may as well, you're awake now. Shit. The other part was right; I was awake. Reluctantly, I got out of bed. Opening the curtains, I saw snow falling. More? Really?? I hadn't seen this much snow since like, forever. It was quite unusual, considering "global warming". I had plenty of time before I needed to leave, so I decided to do a run. Decent run and a hot shower set me up nicely for the day.

Man in kitchen; fully dressed, pacing about nervously. That was me. It was still only 8 o'clock, and I didn't know what to do with myself. *This is stupid*. Ok, you're right. I put my hat, coat, and gloves on and went to the cafe. I'd be super early, but I could chat to Steve for a while to kill the time, rather than staring at the walls here.

Tinkle...

Wow! Busy! The trampled snow outside made me think there'd be a few people in already, but it was *rammed. Lots of people Jack! heheheh*. Shut up! Saturday morning breakfast baps were obviously what most of the village needed. I made my way to the side of the counter, and asked Steve if he could do with a hand.

"Fucking legend. Get in here" He gestured for me to come over. "I need to be in the kitchen, can you work the counter?"

"No worries mate, you go" I waved him away.

"Thank God you're here Jack!" Willow looked stressed "I can't make coffee and take orders at the same time"

"Here to help" I said. I put on an apron and got stuck in.

When the tidal wave of customers finally subsided, we all stood looking at each other. "Holy fuck, that was busy" Steve said

"Yeah, that was mad" said Willow wide-eyed. "Thanks for helping out Jack, you came just at the right time"

"Like I said, happy to help" I said, taking off my apron. "You guys ok?"

"Could do with a sit down" Willow admitted "I'm pooped"

"You guys sit, I'll get the kitchen cleaned up" Steve said, walking off to the little kitchen.

"Coffee?" I asked Willow.

"Sick of the sight of coffee to be honest Jack, water please."

I laughed. "No worries." Got a couple of bottles of water from the fridge, and we sat in the window.

"Your kids seem nice" Willow said

"Yeah, they're great" I responded. She was busy peeling the label off the bottle, obviously something on her mind.

"Something on your mind?" I asked.

A brief pause, then "Can I ask you something"

"Shoot" I said

"Is he a safe bet? I mean, you know him better than anyone, and I just wanted to ask"

"He's safe as houses." I said confidently.

"I've been badly hurt before; I just don't want to..." I cut her off before she could finish.

"Willow, you have nothing to worry about with him; he won't let you down"

"Are you sure?" she didn't seem convinced.

"Let me tell you something..." I started, and continued to tell her the story of Steve's life. When I'd finished a few minutes later, she had tears rolling down her cheeks.

"Oh my god." She said "I didn't know"

"Not many people do. And if they do, it's not spoken about."

"That's why it's called Cafe Jazz" she said "I thought it was a jazz themed cafe when I first saw it"

"Steve hates Jazz" I said laughing. "He's a rock guy through and through."

It went silent. She looked out of the window, lost in thought. After a few moments, she said
"You think I should give him a chance?"
"He deserves happiness. You like each other, it's obvious"
"It is?" she asked
"Yes, trust me" I said.
"Ok. I'll give him a chance" She decided. "Thank you, Jack." She leaned over and kissed me on the cheek, then trotted off to see Steve in the kitchen.
I sat back, feeling pretty proud of myself for helping my friend. *Have a chufty badge Jack*. Cheers inner voice. I had to give away his biggest secret, but it was worth it, and Willow had promised not to mention it to him.
I was still lost in thought, staring out of the window, when Steve plonked down in the chair next to me. "Jesus Steve!"
"I know it was something you said" He said accusatorily "What did you say to sway her to go out with me?"
"I told her the truth" I said hesitantly.
"You what?"
"Cafe Jazz? I told her the truth. She would find out eventually"
He sat and thought for a moment, and I was afraid he was going to react badly.
But, I needn't have worried.
"Thank you" he said, looking me in the eye. "Thank you for doing what I couldn't"
"We look after each other" I said "Regardless of

how hard that can be"

We hugged, and he went off to talk to Willow. "Oh, and Steve..?" I called after him

He turned "Yes mate?"

"Might be time for a change?" I said, gesturing at the name painted on the window.

He looked at the window for a moment, nodded, and walked away. I'd never been more proud of him than I was in that moment. He was ready to move on.

Speaking of which.... Let's talk about "moving on" for a moment. Couple of thoughts:

- How soon is too soon?
- What is the right amount of time you should leave between relationships?
- Is there an accepted norm?
- Should you move on at all?

Last one is easy to answer; yes. Yes, you should. Dwelling on the past is NOT GOOD FOR YOU. That relationship you had? Never coming back. You're never getting back together again. It may take some people longer to come to that realisation, but you will eventually. You have to, for your own sanity.

The first 3 are basically all the same. Answer? Different for everyone. Some people move on straight away, or even before. Some a while later. Some people mo... Hey, you know what? For the first time in this book so far, it's time for a *sub-*

tangent.

How is it different for everyone? Well, it totally depends on your character/personality. What? Think about it. There are three types of people, may be more, but I'm sticking with 3.

These types are:

1. The cold person.

This is the person that can go from loving someone to not loving them in the blink of an eye. Like a light switch; love on, love off. They turn completely cold, and feel nothing for someone, even if they've been together for years.

2. The struggler.

This person struggles to let go. They aren't able to stop loving someone "just like that".

They can't just stop having feelings for someone. It takes time.

How long? Depends on the person.

3. The denier.

This is the person that can never let go. I will love you forever type.

Hello? You split up years ago!! But I still love her. I can't help it.

Which is best? Dunno. Yes, I do; 2 is best.
Think about this story; Helen is a 1 (with a tiny bit of 2), Jack is a thoroughbred 2, and Steve

borderline 3 (mostly 2, but with 3 tendencies).

Which one are *you*?
Think about it for a second, and then think about which one you'd *like* to be. (Especially if you're a 1 or 3)

My two-penny worth?
If you're a 1; good for you. I don't understand 1's, but to each their own.
If you're a 2; welcome to the club. You'll find plenty of company here.
If you're a 3, get help. It's unhealthy. Confide in someone. Anyone.

Let's get back to the cafe; it's about to get to the good part.

Instant nerves; I could see her coming down the street. I looked at my watch; 10 already! *Compose yourself Jack, it's going to be.....* Tinkle...
"Hey you" Big smile.
"Hi" I said, standing.
"She took off her coat, and gave me a hug
"You ok? How long have you been sat here?" she asked jokingly
"Oh, since about 8" I said with a wave of my hand
"Really? Since 8?"
"Yeah, I err..." I faltered. *Ha! Dumbass!* SHUT UP!
"The guy's a hero. He turned up at the right moment; we were super fucking busy, and he rescued us" Steve had appeared out of nowhere.
"Steve, manager, owner, and this guy's best friend"

leans in whispering "only friend if you ask me"
"Thanks mate"
Laughs.
"I'm Chrissy" she said, holding out her hand
Steve shook it "Pleased to meet you at last. Chrissy"
"Same here, I've heard so much about you"
"Oh really? All bad I hope" more laughs. Smooth bastard.
"Oddly enough, I've heard next to nothing about you, but that's Jack for you"
"Steve!!" Willow shouted from behind the counter. "Haven't you got something to do over there somewhere?" I asked waving gesturing towards the kitchen.
"Ok, ok, ok, I know when I'm not wanted" Hands held up in innocence. "Nice to finally meet you Chrissy" he said, then retreated to the kitchen.
"Sorry about him" I said, just loud enough for Steve to catch
"He's lovely" she laughed
"Yes. Yes, he is" I admitted.
"Hi guys, can I get you a drink and something to eat?" Willow stepped up "Pay no attention to him" she said, nodding behind her.
"Hi, yes please. Can I get a gingerbread latte please?"
"Yep, we can do that. Anything to eat?"
"Ooh, cinnamon swirl please if you have one"
"Absolutely. Usual Jack?" turning to me
"Yes, please Willow"
"Back in a sec" she turned and went to work her

magic on the coffee machine.

"You've not told your friend about me?" she asked

"Erm, no. I didn't want to, you know, jinx anything" *Smooth, knob head*

"Bless you. I wouldn't worry too much; you're doing ok"

"So, who do we want to talk about first? Me, or You?" she asked

"You" I said instantly. *Wimp!* Shut up!

Laughs "Ok, let's talk about me"

Willow brought our orders over, and then Chrissy proceeded to tell me all there was to know about Christelle Lenoir. I still love that name. Even now.

Rather than write out the whole thing, let me summarise in factual bullets;

- Christelle Lenoir
- Age 39
- Occupation: Forensic Accountant
- Lives alone in a rather swish looking apartment
- Single
- Orphan
- Loves Italian food
- Hobbies include reading and cycling
- Plays Cello ("average")
- Music lover
- Not a city girl
-

"Forensic accountant? Wow, sounds amazing."

"Nah, it gets boring pretty quick"
"Still sounds amazing."
Her life sounded pretty amazing to be honest; she worked on a freelance basis, and was able to do 90% of her work from a home office, as it's mostly online.
"Hence, I was thinking about moving, to be closer to my Aunt, as I'm the only family she has here in the UK. Her kids both live in New Zealand"
"I like the sound of that" I said, my excitement obvious. *Too obvious?* Shush.
"I bet" smiles.
"Sorry to hear about your parents" I said "Must have been tough"
"Yeah, it was. But, I got myself back on my feet eventually"
Her parents had both been killed in a car accident one evening 12 years ago. They were returning from a night at the theatre, when a truck driver smashed into their car. He was on an overnight drive, and had fallen asleep. The truck had veered over into the oncoming lane and smashed into them head-on.
There was a moment of silence, which was a bit uncomfortable. *Jesus Jack you've done it now.* Thankfully, she rescued the situation.
"So, Jack Beckett, your turn. Tell me all about yourself"
"Me?" I said "Wow, pretty boring in comparison."
Yeah Jack, tell her ALL about you. Shut up!
I told her about growing up here, my job at the

Engineering works, then my career change into content editor. Talked about my relationship with Steve, my lovely kids, and the charming people of the village. She liked that I was a music lover, and we shared a love of Italian food. Running wasn't her thing, but she'd be willing to give it a try if I would help.

"That all sounds pretty amazing Jack, far from boring"
"You're being nice" I said sarcastically.
"No, really. Sounds really lovely, I'm jealous" she argued back with a smile
"One thing though…" she said
"Yes?"
"You haven't mentioned your wife at all" she said
"Ah, yeah. I didn't know if you wanted to hear about her" I answered awkwardly.
"Jack, it's a huge part of your life, and I know how badly it's been affecting you, remember?"
She did. She was right.
"You sure you want to hear?" I asked, just to be sure. I didn't mind talking about it, it just seemed inappropriate at the moment.
"Yes. I want to know all there is to know about you" she said earnestly.
"I'm going to need more coffee in that case" I said. I called over to Willow and asked for another latte.
"You need a refill?" I asked Chrissy
"No, I 'm ok thanks"
And so we sat, for another half hour or so whilst

I told her all about marrying Helen, buying the house, the kids, and the eventual decline into divorce. The letters, the blocking, the child access, the finances; the whole lot. I don't know why, but it felt good to get it all out. She listened intently, and patiently the whole way through. When I had finished, she sat for a moment, in silence.

Shit, you've done it now Jack, she's gonna run a mile! Would she?

"What a bitch" She said eventually. *You're lucky!* Maybe, but I was still surprised by her reaction.

It must have been obvious, because she apologised immediately

"Oh, bugger, I'm sorry" she said apologetically.

"No, no. Don't be, I'm just surprised is all. I thought you were going to do a runner"

She reached across, touched my hand, and looking straight into my eyes, said "I'm going nowhere"

Holy shit. I thought. Holy shit. *What the fu…..* Shut it!

"Thank you" I managed, my heart still pounding.

"But, " she said, looking at her watch "I *do* have to leave, sorry. We're taking Chico to the groomers, so I have to get back to my aunt's."

Relieved, I laughed, and said "Wow, yeah, of course."

"Thank you for a wonderful time Jack" she said, whilst putting her coat on. "It feels good to be able to talk to someone, it's been a while"

"Same here, discounting the idiot in the kitchen…" Laughs. She hugged me, kissed my cheek, and said softly in my ear "You're going to be ok Jack"

I stood in the cafe, watching through the window as she walked away. She turned, smiled, and waved. Then she turned the corner and was gone.
"She's lovely Jack" Willow said, suddenly at my side. "Don't lose her will you?"
"I have no intention of doing so" I said quietly.
"Good" She patted my shoulder and returned to the counter.
"Thanks Willow." I put my coat on "Say goodbye to the lump for me would you?" I said, and walked back home. Felt like I was walking on air.

"Ok, Ok, I get the message" I said to the cat after I walked in. She was curled up in my scarf; it was cold in the house. I put the heating on, and lit the fire. Unsure what to do with myself for the rest of the day, I decided to do some gaming. I fired up the pc and lost myself in some epic tank battles. I could have checked my email and done some work, but I wasn't in the mood. I was on a high, and didn't want to come back down.

The rest of the day/evening was uneventful; I had a call from Mum, some messages from the kids, and Steve asking if it went well. Fridge was pretty bare, and mum's leftovers were probably past their best now. Shit. Managed to fix something for dinner in the end, but I'd have to go shopping tomorrow. Watched a bit of telly and went to bed. Happy.

Headphones stayed where they were; didn't need

help falling asleep tonight.

Zzzzzzzz...

DAY 16

Sunday, 16th of March.

Ugh. Awake stupidly early. 05.28, what's with that?? Hmmm. An intense feeling of dread came over me as I started waking up. It was so bad, it started making me feel sick. Tomorrow. Jesus, I hadn't even gotten out of bed, and my day was fucked already. This was going to be on my mind all day, and I was just going to be ill and have a really shit time. Aaaaaaargh! No! I dragged myself out and made a coffee. Still dark outside. I wasn't loving this. Went up to the office and made a list of jobs for the week; quite a few long videos. It was going to be busy. Very busy. Great. Just what I needed. Great distraction, but not sure I'd be in the frame of mind. Dammit. I could feel I was in a downward spiral, gaining speed, losing altitude. WEEEEEEE! Down we go Jacky boy!
Phone Steve. Now! I got my phone and called. It

rang out. Not today, please…. I called again. And again. And again. No answer. What the fuck? Shit. I need help. Why wasn't he answering? *Jack?* Yes? *Yo, dumbass; its 6 o'clock on a Sunday morning.* Balls.
Ok Jack. Chill. Relax. Breathe. I tried all that. Nothing. The anxiety about tomorrow was taking over.
You know what to do. I did, but didn't like it. I went to the kitchen, opened the draw, and stared at the box for a moment. I hate medication. I don't even take anything for a headache, or a cold. *Think about it Jack, what choice do you have here?* Fuck you inner voice. Stupid thing was; inner voice was right. I took the box, and pushed a pill out of the strip inside. So tiny, but so powerful. I popped it in my mouth, and washed it down with coffee. It would take about an hour to kick in, so I decided to go do a run.

Tangent anyone? Yeah, let's do it. Medication. Anxiety. Mostly anxiety. I have suffered with social anxiety for as long as I can remember. I won't go into the ins and outs of social anxiety; look it up. Let's just say I struggle A LOT in social situations, mostly conversation. I never know what to say, and stand there beating myself up internally. In my previous job, I did a lot of presentations, which were not good for me. I wasn't bad at it, it just took some time to calm down and relax. Doesn't give the best impression though. I'd be ill for days before a presentation, just worried and anxious. It wasn't good. Fed up, I saw my GP about it, and he prescribed Propranolol. An anti-anxiety medication. It's a beta-blocker, dunno what that means; look it up. For me, it reduces my heart rate, and prevents that intense heart beat you get when you're nervous. What does that do? Well, benefits include; no stuttering when talking. Biggest one for me. Likely different results for different people. I can only speak for my own experiences. Although it works well, I don't like taking it. I'm not a medication person.

Anyways, after my run, I showered, and had some toast. Checked my watch; 08.29. Better. Heart rate monitor: 52. Mental wellbeing: not great, but controllable. No feelings of panic. Pill had kicked in. Like I said, powerful pill. I still felt anxious about tomorrow, but not near the levels of earlier. Deep breath….. I was ready for the day.
Ok, what was the plan? Shopping. Of course. Went through the fridge & cupboards and made a list.
Lots of fresh produce; I felt that cooking from scratch would be an extra distraction. And we all know I need distractions. Bags? Check. Car keys? Car keys? Hang on, I'm looking. Check. Ok, let's go. *No. Stop.* What? *Your phone binged. Check it.* Ok. Text from Chrissy.

Her: Morning ☺ do you have any plans for today?

Me: Morning ☺ about to go to the big shop
Her: Big shop?
Me: sorry. Local slang for the big Sainsbury's outside PB
Her: Ah, lol. Want company? I can get my aunt's shopping
Me: Sure ☺
Her: Great ☺
Me: I'll pick you up in 15?
Her: yep, I'll be ready
Me: cool, see you in a bit

Oh, yes. The day had just stepped up a level. I had 15 minutes to make my car look presentable. Nah, what am I saying? You know me by now; my car is immaculate. I checked my appearance quickly, and drove to Mary's house. Small village, so obviously no parking outside the house. It was quiet (even more so than usual…), so I just pulled up outside and waited. Didn't have to wait long; Chrissy opened the door almost immediately, and ran over to the car.

"Hi" she said, whilst getting in. Big smile.

"Hi" I said with a smile of my own.

"Did you mind? Only, I don't get an opportunity to go to the bigger shop very often"

"I'm happy for the company" I said. And I was. Very much so.

It wasn't very far to the shop, about 5 miles or so, so it didn't take us very long to get there. Problem was; it's Sunday. Shop not open till 10. It was just

coming up to 9. Shit.
"Fancy a quick coffee? I forgot the shop doesn't open till 10"
"Sure, that would be nice"
I drove round the corner to the café, and parked around the back.
We walked around to the front, and were about to go in, when Chrissy stopped.
"What's up" I asked
"The window, look, the name has gone" She gestured towards the window. She was right; whereas before it had Café Jazz painted on in ornate lettering, it was now blank.
I laughed. Chrissy just looked at me, puzzled. "What's going on?"
"He's moving on" I said "I'll tell you about it later"
We entered, and Steve came running over
"Mate, you ok?" he asked, very concerned.
"Yes mate, I'm fine. Sorry for the calls"
"I'm sorry I didn't answer. My phone was dead"
"Mate, don't worry. I'm all good now" I reassured him.
"Ok. Good. Did you…" he made a putting-pill-in-mouth gesture
"Yeah, all good dude" I said quickly, hoping Chrissy hadn't seen.
He looked awkward. "Go sit, you'll have to make do with me today I'm afraid, Willow doesn't work Sundays"
"Oh." I turned to Chrissy "You wanna go somewhere else?"

Laughs.

Steve made a show of pretend hurt. "Funny. My coffee isn't that bad. Prick"

"Window is looking good mate" I said mockingly.

"Keep at it knobby. Your idea remember" He said

"Proud of you buddy" I meant it.

He brought the coffees over, and sat with us.

"So, I had an idea for the new name" he said "But, wanted your opinion first"

I took a sip "What's your idea?"

"Going to sound silly, I know, but I was thinking *The Willow Tree Café*"

"Is that not a bit premature?" I asked

"What? No, you idiot. Well, ok, yeah. It is a little nod to Willow I guess. But I was sat here, staring out the window, thinking about what I should call it. Then, I noticed the trees over by the canal. Kind of works both ways right?"

He had a point; this stretch of the canal was lined with willow trees, so it made sense. And he was right; it was a nice nod to Willow. How to impress a girl eh?

"I think it's a good name" Chrissy said with a smile.

"She's right mate, its great"

"Thanks guys, I'll go book the sign writer" He got up and went off to flash up his laptop.

Chrissy looked at me "You know you're going to have to tell me right?"

"Yeah, I know" I said. "Finish your drink and I'll tell you all about it in the car"

We finished up, said bye to Steve, and walked to the

car.

"Right," I said as we drove off "Where do I start…."
I told her the story about Steve and Jasmine.

Like Willow, Chrissy was crying when I'd finished. I parked up in the carpark, which was about half full already. We sat in the car for a few minutes whilst Chrissy "composed herself" as she put it.
"You ok?" I asked
She looked at me, still a bit teary "Yeah, I'm ok. That's really sad"
"I know, it was a tough time."
"Poor guy"
"He's finally moving on now though, which is good for him. It's taken a long time"
"He seems happy" she offered
"He always seems happy on the outside. Inside is a different matter. But, you're right, he is genuinely happier at the moment"
We sat in silence, each lost in our own thoughts
To break the silence I asked "You know he's asked Willow out?"
"No! That's brilliant! She's lovely"
"Yeah, she is. They will be good together" I hoped we would be too, but didn't say that out loud.
"Right, you ready?" It had just gone past 10.
"Yeah, think so."
I got the bags from the back of the car, and we walked into the shop. I picked up a trolley, and we started going through the aisles.
"Lots of nice looking things on your list" she noted

"Entertaining?"

"Well, I was going to ask this girl I fancy over for dinner, but not sure if she'd want to."

"She'd love to" she said "But you'll need this" she picked out an expensive bottle of red and put it in the trolley.

"That's a bit pricey isn't it?" I asked

"You like this girl or not?" she asked teasingly.

"Yeah, I do. A lot"

Smiles.

"Good. I'm sure she'll fall head over heels"

"Dad!"

What? I looked behind us, and saw James running over.

He ran up and hugged me tight

"Hey buddy" I said "What you doing here?" *Lol, this is interesting Jacko!*

"Shopping with mum" he said with a look that said he'd rather be anywhere else.

"Your mum's here?" I asked, alarmed. Shit. Shit. Shit! *Ha! Even better!*

"Yeah, she's here somewhere. But I got bored and wandered off."

He looked at Chrissy. Shit. *Yeah, how you gonna handle this one???*

"Hi, I'm James" he offered his hand

"Hi James, I'm Chrissy" she shook his hand.

"You dad's girlfriend?" he asked

"James!" I said, alarmed

"Don't worry" Chrissy said to me "Would it be ok if

I was?" she asked James

He didn't even need to think "No, it would be a good thing. He's all alone, and I worry about him"

What? I was shocked. *WTF? This isn't right!*

"In that case, yes, I am." she beamed.

What? I was shocked. *She is? When did this happen????*

"Nice one dad" James said "She's tidy"

"Oi!" Chrissy said, laughing

"James!" I said, again.

Few things going through my head:

1. Embarrassed. Like I'd been caught out or something. I really wanted this to happen in a more controlled way.

2. Shocked. One because James was ok with it, two because James's cheek.

3. Confused. What the fuck just happened??????

4. Proud. Proud of my son's maturity and understanding.

5. Happy. Wait, did she just say she was my girlfriend???? What???

6. Scared/Anxious. Where the fuck was Helen?? What if...

Didn't need to worry about the last one...

"Oh, James there you are. I've been...Oh..... Hi Jack."

She came walking up from behind me, my heart sank. Shit. *Oh wow, pass me the popcorn…*

We turned "Hi Helen" I managed, meekly.

She looked at Chrissy, then at me. Fuck. This was bad. This was bad.

"Who's your friend?" looking at me, her look making me feel smaller and smaller.

Chrissy chimed in "Chrissy"

Fuck. Fuck. Fuck.

"Dad's girlfriend" James added proudly

WTF? "James!" I said angrily.

"What?" he said in that typically teenage way.

"Oh…" she said "I had no idea Jack". The look on her face said it all; her world had just collapsed.

"Well, nice to meet you Chrissy. Come on James, we have to go" She turned, and started walking off towards the till.

James hugged me and said "sorry dad".

"Don't worry buddy, was going to happen eventually." I patted his back and kissed his head.

"Bye Chrissy" he said, and left to follow his mother.

"Bye James" she replied with a smile.

Helen turned to see if James was coming, and I could see the tears rolling down her cheeks. I don't know why, and I know I shouldn't have, but I felt sorry for her. If she held some glimmer of hope somewhere deep inside, it just got snuffed out. She now realised she'd lost *everything*. *Well done fuckwit.* Shut up! This wasn't my fault.

"Hey" nudge "You ok?"
"Yeah" I said, snapping out of it
"That was a bit weird" she said, nodding towards Helen.
"You're telling me" I said softly.
"Your son looks just like you, he's lovely" she added encouragingly
"He is, just doesn't engage brain before mouth"
"He's a teenager Jack" she laughed.
"And you…" I began sternly
"What?" she asked, looking a bit worried.
"Girlfriend?" I asked
"Tell me I'm not?" she challenged.
"I can't" I said
"Good, because no wasn't an option" she leaned in and kissed me.

Can't quite recall the rest of the shopping trip, as I was on cloud 9. All thoughts of divorce had been pushed out by this new feeling of being completely and utterly in love. It felt good. Very good.

Before I knew it, I had pulled up outside Mary's, and it was time to go our separate ways. I didn't want her to go.

"Thanks Jack. It was a bit weird, but I think it was going to happen eventually right?"
"Yeah, it was. It wasn't as bad as I thought it was going to be"
"Good. Right, I have my stuff, I'll see you later?" She kissed my cheek.

"Later?" I asked

"Yes, later. That dinner was for me I hope?" she asked with squinted eyes.

"Of course. Yes. Wasn't expecting it to be tonight though" I managed

"Oh. Sorry, I thought…"

I cut her off. "I'm kidding. See you about 6?"

"Perfect" She got out of the car, and went to close the door.

"Wait, you'll need the address!" I called out.

"No, I won't" she winked, closed the door, and walked off.

Gonna pause it here for a sec.

Not going to lie; I tried 2 different story lines here. One was me, bumping into Helen and both kids in the shop, the other me, bumping into Helen and James in the shop. But with Chrissy. I was in two minds whether I wanted the kid(s) to see Jack with Chrissy at this point, as he had made a big deal of not wanting the kids to see him with another woman. Although he had been on his own for 8 months, he felt it wasn't appropriate until the divorce was final. Think of that what you will, but remember from yesterday; he's a 2.

I wrote both story lines, but finally settled for option 2. Although I already had the last lines of this book in mind (it involved introducing the kids to Chrissy), the story where they bumped into Helen and James just read better. I was toying with the idea of putting the alt story line in an appendix, but scrapped it; it didn't read right, didn't flow with the story.

Right choice? Who knows?

In the meantime:

I got back to the house, and was running around in a mild panic; shit, she's coming HERE. TONIGHT.
The house was immaculate, of course, but I was worried nevertheless. I wanted to make the right impression. Also, I hadn't planned on cooking for two. I needed to find something new to make with what I had. *Calm down Jack. Calm down. You want to take another pill?* "No!" I said out loud. No, I didn't; I'd be ok. I grabbed a pen and paper and wrote it out:

Stop panicking.
Why are you panicking?
What reason is there for panic?
Calm it down.
Your house is clean, and looks great.
The food will be fine.
Who cares what the house looks like? It's a family home, not going to change
The food will be fine

I sat and read what I had written, then scrunched up the paper and threw it in the recycle bin.
Thought about calling Steve, but no; I would do this by myself. Idea: I went to the stereo and put the MiniDisc labelled "Feeder" in the player, and

selected Just a Day. Volume up. Danced around like an idiot until the song ended. Felt good. Felt better. Much better.

Minor tangent:
For those who don't know what a MiniDisc is; it's a format that came from Sony in the early 90's. An attempt to evolve the Cassette (look it up if you need to) into the digital age. It was a small disc, protected from scratching. (CDs scratched easily, and the early CD players couldn't cope with that) Look it up. Better than CD in my opinion. Sadly faded away.
Just FYI, my stereo has a record player, tape deck (cassettes), MiniDisc deck, and a cd player. I also have a reel to reel and an 8-track player in the attic. (Again; look it up if you need to)
Call me retro. Or old. Whatever…. It's great.

After jumping round like a muppet, I went and had a shower. Took me a while to pick the right outfit, and then had one last check around the house. All was good. You have 1 hour; get cooking.
I was going to make a lasagne and bake some fresh bread to go with it. Music playing, I was off. Didn't hear the doorbell ring, I was too engrossed in cooking. My phone buzzed in my pocket. Message from Chrissy: "Open the door". Shit. I ran to the door and opened it.
"Finally!" she said "It's freezing out here!"
"Sorry, I was busy in the kitchen. Come, come in"
She came in, and took off her coat. *Holy crap Jack,*

she's a stunner!
"Oh! Lovely and warm in here" she said, from what seemed like 10000 miles away.
She looked fantastic, beautiful, wearing a knee length floral dress with brown boots. No wonder she was cold. Her hair was tied back, and she had minimal makeup on. She looked amazing.
Out of your league boy! Fuck you, inner voice!
"Hello?" she waved her hand in front of my eyes "Earth to Jack"
"Sorry" I said "you look amazing"
"Thank you." she said coyly, which seemed totally out of character. She was normally so confident. I guess even the most confident people have a weakness. Surely not vanity Chrissy?

We walked into the kitchen, and she looked around. "Wow, nice kitchen"
"Thanks. My favourite room in the house"
"I can see why" still sounding impressed.
"Drink?" I asked.
"Yes please, wine? Something smells good. You making bread?"
"Yeah, I love fresh bread"
"I'm impressed."
I poured her a glass of wine and handed it to her
"Cheers"
"Cheers" she said, and we clinked glasses.
"Nice wine" she said approvingly
"It's not bad" I said with a wink.
She put the glass down "So, how about a tour?"

"Of the house? Sure". I checked the oven, and took her on a tour of my home.

Tour over, we returned to the kitchen.
"I love your house" she said "It's beautifully done"
"Thanks. Took a while, but I think it's getting there" I replied modestly
"Your home office is amazing, so spacious. I have to make do with my kitchen table" She joked
"Used to be the bedroom, but I decided the space was better used differently following, well, you know" *Before what? Your wife realising you were a loser??* Fuck off!
"Gotcha" she said knowingly. "You're so lucky. A place like this would cost a fortune in the city"
"Right place, right time I guess" I replied with a shrug of the shoulders.
The oven started beeping "Time to take the bread out"
I opened the oven and took out the bread. "Wow, that looks great" she said "Not sure my cooking skills are even remotely the same as yours" Laughs.
"I've had plenty of time to myself to practice I guess"
"Hopefully you'll have better ways to fill your time now" she added with a smile
"I've already forgotten how to cook..." I joked.
"Charmer. You're doing ok."
"You want to sit? I'll bring the food over" I pulled out a chair for her, and she sat. I brought the food over, and served.

"Thank you. This all smells fantastic" she said earnestly.
And so we ate, and had another glass of wine. We chatted the whole time about our work, my kids, how she had put her flat up for sale, Steve and Willow, and many other things.

Wait! She's put her flat up for sale?
"You put your flat up for sale?" I asked
"Hmm, yeah, did it Friday. Told you, I was looking to move closer to Aunt Mary"

Yes, she did. Remember? I asked if she had found somewhere she liked, and she said there were a few flats over the canal where my parents live. But she wasn't in a rush, her aunt had said she could live with her for as long as she wanted.

We finished our meal, and I tidied up whilst she told me more about her job. She poured more wine, and we went and sat in the lounge.
"So, " she said "Big day tomorrow. You ready for it?"
"Yeah. I think so. I was terrified about it, you know? But now, I can't wait to have it finally over and done with."
"I can understand that. Must have been a tough time for you."
"Yeah, it has. But that's all done now."

We chatted some more about the kids, and how she would love to meet Elsie.
"I'm sure that'll happen soon enough" I said.

"Hopefully I'll be seeing a lot more of the kids from now on" *You hope!* Sod off, I *know*.
"Cheers to that" Clink.
"Right, " she said, looking at her watch "I have to go. Sorry. I have an early work meeting tomorrow"
"No problem" I said "I have a tonne of work to get through this week, so could do with getting to bed on time" *Make a move!* What? Shut up! *Wimp.*
We stood, and walked out to the hall. I held her coat, and she put it on.
"I had a really good time Jack, thank you" she said
"Me too, being with you feels good" I responded.
"Same here. Please let me know how it goes tomorrow ok? I'm only across the village"
"I will. As soon as I hear, you'll hear"
"Goodnight Jack" she said, and we kissed.
"Goodnight Christelle"
I closed the door after watching her walk down the road, and stood for a moment, thinking about what had just happened. With a huge smile on my face.
She is great, I thought, and beautiful, and understanding, and supportive, and keen to meet my kids. She's perfect. And I would do everything I could to keep her.

On a high, I went up to bed.

I had a big day tomorrow. It could go either way, but I was confident I would stay positive, and not crash into a pit of depression. This whole saga would come to an end, the divorce finalised; I would be able to move on with my life. Hopefully, the kids would be here more, and I would be able to introduce them to Chrissy in due time. Well, just Elsie at least. I was sure James had probably told her all about his meeting her though.

Needed to ensure I stayed positive. The huge volume of work would hopefully keep my mind occupied enough to stop it drifting towards the dark. Stay positive Jack You got this. And you know what? I think I did.

I put my headphones on and took a Hansom to Victorian London where Mr Holmes guided me from 221b Baker Street to the land of zzzzzzzz's. Goodnight……

DAY 17

Monday, 17th of March.

Woke up way before the alarm. Full of anxiety already. Here to fuck you up pal! No, not going to happen. You're funny Jacky boy. Hit me with your best shot. I got up, went downstairs, and took a pill. Without any hesitation; today was not a day for fucking about. What the hell you doing? No!
Sod off. Could really do without you niggling at me all day, it's going to be bad enough as it is.
Did a run, showered, made coffee, and went to work. There really was a lot of work to get through this week, I needed to be on my game here.

If I needed positivity, it came in buckets:

Checked my emails. Lots from clients. All good. Lots of praise and thanks for the great work. Also, email from my newest client; contracts all received and processed. Welcome aboard! Lots of corporate stuff to complete, HR on boarding courses, setting up my company account, choosing a benefits package, and a few other bits and pieces. They would give me a week before sending me work, so I could get all the corporate stuff out of the way. Don't get the wrong impression; this isn't a huge global company we're talking about. It's a family business, but had grown to the point where a "big-business" structure was required. They had a reputation for looking after their employees VERY well though. Which was great. I needed security. In addition, I was entitled to employee discounts in their store (new guitar Jack?), and would be receiving a sign-on bonus as a welcome gift. What? Wow. Probably vouchers, but; wow. All good news. Did wonders for my mood. Checked my watch; heart rate looking good. Fuck you anxiety.

12 Videos to do. Let's get stuck in.
I got to work. Phone buzzed several times throughout the morning; Mum, Steve, Chrissy, Elsie, James. All checking to see if I was ok. And asking for money in the kid's case....
I told them all I was fine, and no news yet. Kids wanted to know if they could come over after school; of course! More positivity.

Let's see how it stacks up at the moment:

Positives:	Negatives:
Work praise	Anxiety

17 DAYS

New employee awesomeness   Divorce
Kids coming
Chrissy is my girlfriend!
Surrounded by caring, loving people.

Scale tipped in the positive direction; fuck you negativity!
I went down to the kitchen, put some music on, and made some toast for breakfast.
Mental note: Running out of marmalade.
Behind me: doorbell.
I almost dropped my plate. Keep it together!!!!
I opened the door; postman.
"Morning Jack, got one that needs a signature"
He scanned the barcode, then handed me the little machine & stylus, and I signed accordingly.
"Thanks mate"
He handed me the envelope, and another small bundle of letters.
"Have a great day Jack, take care"
"Thanks Jeff, you too"
I closed the door. My heart tried it's hardest to pound, but the Propranolol was doing its job. I was nervous, but not the wreck I would have been without it.

I looked at the envelope: Peterborough Combined Court. This is it Jack; end of the road.
I opened it, and removed the contents. Inside was a cover letter, and what I'd been waiting for; Certificate of Decree Absolute. Fuck. It was over. My previous life, my marriage, all the love and

great experiences; now just a piece of paper. Did it make me feel sad? No. It made me happy. This had been a living nightmare for almost 9 months now, and I was just happy to have it done with.

Tangent:
When you receive this document, it's easy to spiral out of control. Don't. Read the last paragraph above. All that stuff is true: "...previous life, my marriage, all the love and great experiences; now just a piece of paper." Think about it, it is. Or is it? Well, now it starts getting complicated. Especially if you have re-married, or just have a new partner.

Are you allowed to think of your marriage afterwards? Of course. Only a machine would be able to delete memories/experiences from its memory banks. Throughout the rest of your life, you will see something, or experience something that brings back a memory or a feeling. And you know what? It's perfectly ok, and natural. You've just spent x amount of years loving someone, living with them, sharing experiences with them, raising children with them, etc. All this will stay with you forever. As you age, you will naturally forget a lot, but all it takes is an object, trip, song, or whatever to bring it back to life.

Should your new wife/partner be ok with this? Depends on the person. Insecurity in second marriages is high, naturally. As long as your new partner has been made aware that although you may mention it occasionally, it really means nothing, you might be ok. And that depends on how YOU are as a person. Open/Honest or Closed/Secretive. Personally, I DO share some things with my new wife. Because I believe in honesty. Sometimes she gets a little off, but deep down, I think she knows that the path back to the ex is forever closed & destroyed. I have more than re-assured her of this.

Interesting point; insecurity in second marriages. What do I mean by that? Simple. Your wife will naturally harbour fears that you will reconcile with your ex, and drop her like a rock. She'll be left on her own. Working through this again, depends on personalities. I can only speak for myself. I made a BIG deal of letting her know I was going to be completely honest with her, and expected the same in return. If she had concerns, tell me and we can work through them. And vice-versa. Keeping stuff like this inside leads to festering resentment and will lead to bad things.
Be open.
Be honest.

So, back to the story. I had read the letter. "Mr Beckett, please find attached…bla…bla…, Sincerely,…bla."
I took a deep breath, and held it in for a bit. Then slowly exhaled; breathing out all the ill feelings and badness. From now on, I wouldn't let it get me

down. I didn't need to; I was no longer married.
Bang tidy.
As an aside; I never heard from Helen regarding her feelings about the divorce being finalised. Not that I was too concerned. It was over, she was no longer anything to do with me.

I called Mum: She was happy for me. Happy that it was finally over. They would pop over in the morning for a cup of tea and a chat.

I called Steve: Many (MANY) expletives. But the gist is: I'm happy for you mate, it's done. Pint and chat required. - Deffo.

I called Chrissy: She was very happy that I was in a good place, and could finally move on. And she would meet me later in the Café if that was ok. - Of course. We talked about another matter for a bit, and agreed to meet at 1700.

I put the certificate and letter back in the envelope, and put it away in my file cabinet. Never to be seen again hopefully. I wasn't going to need it for anything.
Happy, and proud of myself, I went back to work.

I finished 3 out of 12 videos. Then it was time to shut down and get ready; the kids would be here in 30. I checked their rooms, made sure I had enough bread & milk, and had a general tidy round.
By the time I'd finished that, the doorbell rang;

they were here. My heart started pounding. Not from anxiety, but from love; I couldn't wait to hold them in my arms.

They were super excited to see me, and the feeling was mutual. We hugged, and had a long chat.

An even bigger, more anxious experience was about to happen. We walked to the caf. "Look dad, " Elsie said, pointing at the window "Uncle Steve has changed the name"

She was right; bright, bold lettering, it now said "Willow Tree Cafe". Well done mate. Well done.

We went inside, my heart racing, anxiety rising.

"Hey guys" Steve called from behind the counter "Get over here and give Uncle Steve a hug!" They laughed and ran over for hugs.

I went over, and got a massive hug myself.

"You ok?"

"I will be in a minute mate" I said.

"Ah. Good luck" he said with a knowing look.

"Hey you two, leave Steve alone now, come on let's sit down" Heart pounding.

We walked over to my usual table. Someone was already sat there

Heart about to explode….Deep breath. Go….

"Guys, I'd like you to meet Chrissy"

The End.

POSTSCRIPT

Wow. It's done. Complete. Finished. Out of my head, onto the page.

I hope you read this book and had a bit of a laugh. Apart from the serious stuff, it was meant to have a slightly funny "comic relief" feel to it. Especially in the banter between Jack and Steve.

It was supposed to be a story of despair, with all the tangents that go with it, but also a story of hope. Hope. For you. Hope that it will get better. Perhaps it already has, and you recognise some of yourself in the character Jack.

I will say that when I started writing, I didn't have a full story idea in mind. Just a concept; a guy and a divorce. The story and characters developed themselves as I typed.

I had a great time writing this. It wasn't supposed to grow into something where I felt "Hey, I could do a sequel to this". But; it has. I think that the characters are strong enough for a follow-on story.

But that's in the future.

Till then,

Look after yourself,

Seek help if you need to,
And thank you for reading.
Mike, 10 March 2024.

ACKNOWLEDGEMENT

Thank you ever so much to my proof reader Sarah.

Super patience, and super critical.
Both qualities greatly appreciated.

Thank you

Printed in Great Britain
by Amazon